Jhumpa Lahiri

was born in London of Bengali parents, and grew up in Rhode Island, USA. Her stories have appeared in many American journals, including the *New Yorker*. *Interpreter of Maladies*, her first published collection, won the Pulitzer Prize 2000 for Fiction, the *New Yorker* Prize for Best First Book, the PEN/Hemingway Award and was shortlisted for the *Los Angeles Times* Award. Jhumpa Lahiri lives in New York.

From the British reviews for *Interpreter of Maladies*:

'Jhumpa Lahiri's strength as a writer stems partly from her ability to delineate in telling detail the mores of both societies... There are at the moment many good writers of Indian origin who recall with troubled nostalgia a past they do not want to return to but somehow hope to resolve by explaining it in fictional form. Lahiri joins the ranks of those whose work goes further and illuminates human nature in general... So far she has written only short stories. From the evidence of *Interpreter of Maladies* she has enough twists in her plots, confrontations and comic possibilities to sustain a longer form.'

TLS

'The simplicity of language and narrative reminds you of Raymond Carver, with the same eye for detail: Lahiri evokes beautifully the scenario of a young couple living in Boston still getting to know each other after their arranged marriage. But then she jumps to Bengal for "The Treatment of Bidi Holder", about an ill woman who thinks sex is the cure. And her language changes as easily as the location – now Lahiri is florid, rhythmic, and no stranger to a loaded simile... As someone brought up in America, she's finely attuned to the experience of the Indian out of India. Everything that you wanted to know about the immigrant experience can be found in these pages.'

day Herald

D1437683

From the US reviews:

'Lahiri is a writer of uncommon elegance and poise, and with *Interpreter of Maladies* she has made a precocious debut.'

New York Times

'These stories begin in America but, like the letters and histories they reveal, reach back to India. Stewed lamb, lentils, and mango juice are like Proustian madeleines to Lahiri's characters. Their memories and stories are meals to be eaten, at once bitter and sweet, as an attempt at bridging the two worlds together... [These stories] reward the reader with their equipoise of beauty and harsh truths about the politics of borderland existence.'

Boston Book Review

'Like Carver, Lahiri writes about a young couple who have fallen out of love and are playing a bittersweet game amid the detritus of their life together. Like Hemingway, she writes about a tour guide who has more heart than the bourgeois couple who hire him. Like Isherwood, she writes about an earnest young man studying his landlady, whose calcified habits at first unnerve him and then draw out his tenderness. But none of her stories is apprentice work. Lahiri revises these scenarios with unexpected twists, and to each she brings her distinctive insight into the ways that human affections both sustain and defy the cultural forms that try to enclose them.

Lahiri breathes unpredictable life into the page, and the reader finishes each story re-seduced, wishing he could spend a whole novel with its characters. There is nothing accidental about her success; her plots are as elegantly constructed as a fine proof in mathematics. To use the word Sanjeev eventually applies to Twinkle, Lahiri is "wow."'

New York Times Book Review

'The experience of being foreign and the need for connection both mark Lahiri's outstanding debut collection of short stories.'

New York

'*Interpreter of Maladies* is a testament to Lahiri's versatility as a writer: she changes cultural perspective as easily as a bilingual speaker shifts from language to language... These stories are at once subtle and informative, filling cultural gaps with the invisible ease granted only to writers of foreign heritage and exceptional skill... Interlaced with telling detail, these disparate stories reveal Lahiri's craft, her careful choices, and her exquisite language.'
Boston Phoenix

'Lahiri's touch is delicate yet assured, leaving no room for flubbed notes or forced epiphanies.'
Los Angeles Times Book Review

'Storytelling of surpassing kindness and skill.'
San Francisco Chronicle

'Aside from Lahiri's eloquence, there are two things, seemingly at odds with one another, that make this a stunning literary debut. One is her spectacular ability to portray characters who are unassuming, if not passive. The other is her talent for making stories featuring these same characters remarkably suspenseful.'
Newsday

'Lahiri's language is uncluttered; she's sparing with metaphor, and the riches accumulate unobtrusively.'
Newsweek

'What makes Lahiri's debut collection of stories stand out is precisely its quality of unexpected ordinariness. It's not that these tales of Americanized Indians are themselves ordinary... It's the familiarity of the world Lahiri captures...that distinguishes the books. Brimming with promise, Lahiri has a knack for exposing the silent sacrifices and small moments of ridiculousness of people navigating between two worlds.'
Time Out NY

From the Indian reviews:

'Lahiri's depiction of characters and her superb storytelling skills make for engaging reading. You're drawn at once to the sheer humanness of these souls, recognising in their sorrows, joys, expectations and dilemmas some of your own... Lahiri throws in generous doses of humour, so that the stories entertain just as they illuminate. But the real measure of her nine short stories is the quality of the writing – flawless prose which makes an impact through spot-on, detailed observations laced with humour and irony. Definitely worth your while. And your money.'   *Outlook*

'Delightfully unpretentious, shorn of the kind of forced mixed metaphors that have now become the trademark in contemporary Indo-Anglian writing, Lahiri's anthology of short stories comes straight from the heart... Rich in irony, shimmering with gentle wit, *Interpreter of Maladies* is a wry look at the way of the world. Which is no different in Bengal than it is in Boston.'
New Delhi Economic Times

'These short stories of Indians in exile, of the vagaries of contemporary life, will induce many readers to wonder, and some to weep.'   *Cosmopolitan*

'The sense of just-rightness, of chiselled precision and classical restraint are the most striking features of this book... In her best stories, Lahiri's skill with the unspoken, the unmentioned, touches off hidden springs of cultural memory and history which resonate within the slightest incidents... Lahiri's tales are a repository of old-fashioned virtues. Tightly knit, gripping narrative, sharply outlined and varied characters, a refreshingly unsentimental approach, irony, humour and impersonal compassion – these make for a clean-limbed classic quality a little unusual in an age of flamboyance.'   *Calcutta Telegraph*

JHUMPA LAHIRI

Interpreter of Maladies

Stories

Flamingo
An Imprint of HarperCollins*Publishers*
77–85 Fulham Palace Road, Hammersmith, London W6 8JB
Flamingo is a registered trade mark of HarperCollins Publishers Limited

www.**fire**and**water**.com
Published by Flamingo 2000
17 19 18 16

First published in Great Britain in 1999 by Flamingo
First published in the USA in 1999 by Houghton Mifflin Company

Some of the stories in this collection have appeared elsewhere, in a slightly
different form: 'A Temporary Matter' in the *New Yorker*; 'When Mr Pirzada
Came to Dine' in the *Louisville Review*; 'Interpreter of Maladies' in the
Agni Review; 'A Real Durwan' in the *Harvard Review*; 'Mrs Sen's'
in *Salamander*; 'This Blessed House' in *Epoch*; and 'The Treatment
of Bibi Haldar' in *Story Quarterly*.

Photograph of Jhumpa Lahiri © Jerry Bauer

ISBN 0 00 655179 3

Printed and bound by Clays Ltd, St Ives plc

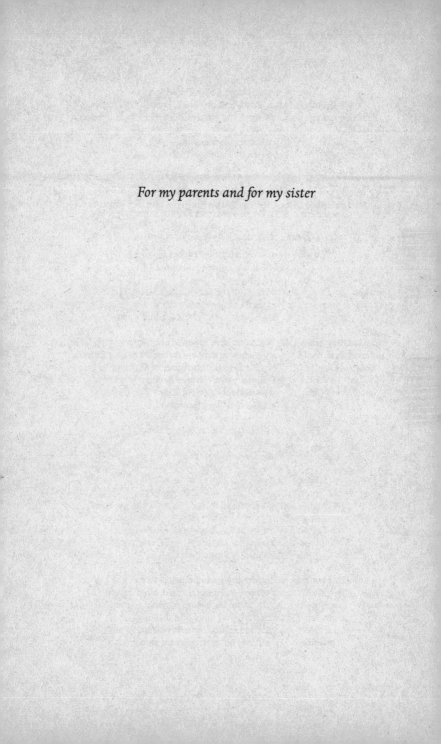

For my parents and for my sister

WITH THANKS TO

the Fine Arts Work Center in Provincetown,
Janet Silver, and Cindy Klein Roche

Contents

A Temporary Matter

THE NOTICE INFORMED THEM that it was a temporary matter: for five days their electricity would be cut
off for one hour, beginning at eight P.M. A line had
gone down in the last snowstorm, and the repairmen were
going to take advantage of the milder evenings to set it right.
The work would affect only the houses on the quiet tree-lined
street, within walking distance of a row of brick-faced stores
and a trolley stop, where Shoba and Shukumar had lived for
three years.

"It's good of them to warn us," Shoba conceded after reading the notice aloud, more for her own benefit than Shukumar's. She let the strap of her leather satchel, plump with files,
slip from her shoulders, and left it in the hallway as she walked
into the kitchen. She wore a navy blue poplin raincoat over
gray sweatpants and white sneakers, looking, at thirty-three,
like the type of woman she'd once claimed she would never
resemble.

She'd come from the gym. Her cranberry lipstick was visible only on the outer reaches of her mouth, and her eyeliner
had left charcoal patches beneath her lower lashes. She used to

look this way sometimes, Shukumar thought, on mornings after a party or a night at a bar, when she'd been too lazy to wash her face, too eager to collapse into his arms. She dropped a sheaf of mail on the table without a glance. Her eyes were still fixed on the notice in her other hand. "But they should do this sort of thing during the day."

"When I'm here, you mean," Shukumar said. He put a glass lid on a pot of lamb, adjusting it so only the slightest bit of steam could escape. Since January he'd been working at home, trying to complete the final chapters of his dissertation on agrarian revolts in India. "When do the repairs start?"

"It says March nineteenth. Is today the nineteenth?" Shoba walked over to the framed corkboard that hung on the wall by the fridge, bare except for a calendar of William Morris wallpaper patterns. She looked at it as if for the first time, studying the wallpaper pattern carefully on the top half before allowing her eyes to fall to the numbered grid on the bottom. A friend had sent the calendar in the mail as a Christmas gift, even though Shoba and Shukumar hadn't celebrated Christmas that year.

"Today then," Shoba announced. "You have a dentist appointment next Friday, by the way."

He ran his tongue over the tops of his teeth; he'd forgotten to brush them that morning. It wasn't the first time. He hadn't left the house at all that day, or the day before. The more Shoba stayed out, the more she began putting in extra hours at work and taking on additional projects, the more he wanted to stay in, not even leaving to get the mail, or to buy fruit or wine at the stores by the trolley stop.

Six months ago, in September, Shukumar was at an academic conference in Baltimore when Shoba went into labor, three weeks before her due date. He hadn't wanted to go to the conference, but she had insisted; it was important to make contacts, and he would be entering the job market next year. She told him that she had his number at the hotel, and a copy of his schedule and flight numbers, and she had arranged with her friend Gillian for a ride to the hospital in the event of an emergency. When the cab pulled away that morning for the airport, Shoba stood waving good-bye in her robe, with one arm resting on the mound of her belly as if it were a perfectly natural part of her body.

Each time he thought of that moment, the last moment he saw Shoba pregnant, it was the cab he remembered most, a station wagon, painted red with blue lettering. It was cavernous compared to their own car. Although Shukumar was six feet tall, with hands too big ever to rest comfortably in the pockets of his jeans, he felt dwarfed in the back seat. As the cab sped down Beacon Street, he imagined a day when he and Shoba might need to buy a station wagon of their own, to cart their children back and forth from music lessons and dentist appointments. He imagined himself gripping the wheel, as Shoba turned around to hand the children juice boxes. Once, these images of parenthood had troubled Shukumar, adding to his anxiety that he was still a student at thirty-five. But that early autumn morning, the trees still heavy with bronze leaves, he welcomed the image for the first time.

A member of the staff had found him somehow among the identical convention rooms and handed him a stiff square of stationery. It was only a telephone number, but Shukumar knew it was the hospital. When he returned to Boston it was over. The baby had been born dead. Shoba was lying on a bed, asleep, in a private room so small there was barely enough space to stand beside her, in a wing of the hospital they hadn't been to on the tour for expectant parents. Her placenta had weakened and she'd had a cesarean, though not quickly enough. The doctor explained that these things happen. He smiled in the kindest way it was possible to smile at people known only professionally. Shoba would be back on her feet in a few weeks. There was nothing to indicate that she would not be able to have children in the future.

These days Shoba was always gone by the time Shukumar woke up. He would open his eyes and see the long black hairs she shed on her pillow and think of her, dressed, sipping her third cup of coffee already, in her office downtown, where she searched for typographical errors in textbooks and marked them, in a code she had once explained to him, with an assortment of colored pencils. She would do the same for his dissertation, she promised, when it was ready. He envied her the specificity of her task, so unlike the elusive nature of his. He was a mediocre student who had a facility for absorbing details without curiosity. Until September he had been diligent if not dedicated, summarizing chapters, outlining arguments on pads of yellow lined paper. But now he would lie in their bed until he grew bored, gazing at his side of the closet which Shoba always left partly open, at the row of the tweed jackets and corduroy trousers he would not have to choose from to teach his classes that semester. After the baby died it was too late to withdraw from his teaching duties. But his adviser had arranged things so that he had the spring semester to himself. Shukumar was in his sixth year of graduate school. "That and the summer should give you a good push," his adviser had said. "You should be able to wrap things up by next September."

But nothing was pushing Shukumar. Instead he thought of how he and Shoba had become experts at avoiding each other in their three-bedroom house, spending as much time on separate floors as possible. He thought of how he no longer looked forward to weekends, when she sat for hours on the sofa with her colored pencils and her files, so that he feared that putting on a record in his own house might be rude. He thought of how long it had been since she looked into his eyes and smiled, or whispered his name on those rare occasions they still reached for each other's bodies before sleeping.

In the beginning he had believed that it would pass, that he and Shoba would get through it all somehow. She was only thirty-three. She was strong, on her feet again. But it wasn't a consolation. It was often nearly lunchtime when Shukumar would finally pull himself out of bed and head downstairs to the coffeepot, pouring out the extra bit Shoba left for him, along with an empty mug, on the countertop.

Shukumar gathered onion skins in his hands and let them drop into the garbage pail, on top of the ribbons of fat he'd trimmed from the lamb. He ran the water in the sink, soaking the knife and the cutting board, and rubbed a lemon half along his fingertips to get rid of the garlic smell, a trick he'd learned from Shoba. It was seven-thirty. Through the window he saw the sky, like soft black pitch. Uneven banks of snow still lined the sidewalks, though it was warm enough for people to walk about without hats or gloves. Nearly three feet had fallen in the last storm, so that for a week people had to walk single file, in narrow trenches. For a week that was Shukumar's excuse for not leaving the house. But now the trenches were widening, and water drained steadily into grates in the pavement.

"The lamb won't be done by eight," Shukumar said. "We may have to eat in the dark."

"We can light candles," Shoba suggested. She unclipped her hair, coiled neatly at her nape during the days, and pried the sneakers from her feet without untying them. "I'm going to shower before the lights go," she said, heading for the staircase. "I'll be down."

Shukumar moved her satchel and her sneakers to the side of the fridge. She wasn't this way before. She used to put her coat on a hanger, her sneakers in the closet, and she paid bills as soon as they came. But now she treated the house as if it were a hotel. The fact that the yellow chintz armchair in the living room clashed with the blue-and-maroon Turkish carpet no longer bothered her. On the enclosed porch at the back of the house, a crisp white bag still sat on the wicker chaise, filled with lace she had once planned to turn into curtains.

While Shoba showered, Shukumar went into the downstairs bathroom and found a new toothbrush in its box beneath the sink. The cheap, stiff bristles hurt his gums, and he spit some blood into the basin. The spare brush was one of many stored in a metal basket. Shoba had bought them once when they were on sale, in the event that a visitor decided, at the last minute, to spend the night.

It was typical of her. She was the type to prepare for surprises, good and bad. If she found a skirt or a purse she liked she bought two. She kept the bonuses from her job in a separate bank account in her name. It hadn't bothered him. His own mother had fallen to pieces when his father died, abandoning the house he grew up in and moving back to Calcutta, leaving Shukumar to settle it all. He liked that Shoba was different. It astonished him, her capacity to think ahead. When she used to do the shopping, the pantry was always stocked with extra bottles of olive and corn oil, depending on whether they were cooking Italian or Indian. There were endless boxes of pasta in all shapes and colors, zippered sacks of basmati rice, whole sides of lambs and goats from the Muslim butchers at Haymarket, chopped up and frozen in endless plastic bags.

Every other Saturday they wound through the maze of stalls Shukumar eventually knew by heart. He watched in disbelief as she bought more food, trailing behind her with canvas bags as she pushed through the crowd, arguing under the morning sun with boys too young to shave but already missing teeth, who twisted up brown paper bags of artichokes, plums, gingerroot, and yams, and dropped them on their scales, and tossed them to Shoba one by one. She didn't mind being jostled, even when she was pregnant. She was tall, and broad-shouldered, with hips that her obstetrician assured her were made for childbearing. During the drive back home, as the car curved along the Charles, they invariably marveled at how much food they'd bought.

It never went to waste. When friends dropped by, Shoba would throw together meals that appeared to have taken half a day to prepare, from things she had frozen and bottled, not cheap things in tins but peppers she had marinated herself with rosemary, and chutneys that she cooked on Sundays, stirring boiling pots of tomatoes and prunes. Her labeled mason jars lined the shelves of the kitchen, in endless sealed pyramids, enough, they'd agreed, to last for their grandchildren to taste. They'd eaten it all by now. Shukumar had been going through their supplies steadily, preparing meals for the two of them, measuring out cupfuls of rice, defrosting bags of meat day after day. He combed through her cookbooks every afternoon, following her penciled instructions to use two teaspoons of ground coriander seeds instead of one, or red lentils instead of yellow. Each of the recipes was dated, telling the first time they had eaten the dish together. April 2, cauliflower with fennel. January 14, chicken with almonds and sultanas. He had no memory of eating those meals, and yet there they were, recorded in her neat proofreader's hand. Shukumar enjoyed cooking now. It was the one thing that made him feel productive. If it weren't for him, he knew, Shoba would eat a bowl of cereal for her dinner.

Tonight, with no lights, they would have to eat together. For months now they'd served themselves from the stove, and he'd taken his plate into his study, letting the meal grow cold on his desk before shoving it into his mouth without pause, while Shoba took her plate to the living room and watched game shows, or proofread files with her arsenal of colored pencils at hand.

At some point in the evening she visited him. When he heard her approach he would put away his novel and begin typing sentences. She would rest her hands on his shoulders and stare with him into the blue glow of the computer screen. "Don't work too hard," she would say after a minute or two, and head off to bed. It was the one time in the day she sought him out, and yet he'd come to dread it. He knew it was something she forced herself to do. She would look around the walls of the room, which they had decorated together last summer with a border of marching ducks and rabbits playing trumpets and drums. By the end of August there was a cherry crib under the window, a white changing table with mint-green knobs, and a rocking chair with checkered cushions. Shukumar had disassembled it all before bringing Shoba back from the hospital, scraping off the rabbits and ducks with a spatula. For some reason the room did not haunt him the way it haunted Shoba. In January, when he stopped working at his carrel in the library, he set up his desk there deliberately, partly because the room soothed him, and partly because it was a place Shoba avoided.

Shukumar returned to the kitchen and began to open drawers. He tried to locate a candle among the scissors, the eggbeaters and whisks, the mortar and pestle she'd bought in a bazaar in Calcutta, and used to pound garlic cloves and cardamom pods, back when she used to cook. He found a flashlight, but no batteries, and a half-empty box of birthday candles. Shoba had thrown him a surprise birthday party last May. One hundred and twenty people had crammed into the house — all the friends and the friends of friends they now systematically avoided. Bottles of vinho verde had nested in a bed of ice in the bathtub. Shoba was in her fifth month, drinking ginger ale from a martini glass. She had made a vanilla cream cake with custard and spun sugar. All night she kept Shukumar's long fingers linked with hers as they walked among the guests at the party.

Since September their only guest had been Shoba's mother. She came from Arizona and stayed with them for two months after Shoba returned from the hospital. She cooked dinner every night, drove herself to the supermarket, washed their clothes, put them away. She was a religious woman. She set up a small shrine, a framed picture of a lavender-faced goddess and a plate of marigold petals, on the bedside table in the guest room, and prayed twice a day for healthy grandchildren in the future. She was polite to Shukumar without being friendly. She folded his sweaters with an expertise she had learned from her job in a department store. She replaced a missing button on his winter coat and knit him a beige and brown scarf, presenting it to him without the least bit of ceremony, as if he had only dropped it and hadn't noticed. She never talked to him about Shoba; once, when he mentioned the baby's death, she looked up from her knitting, and said, "But you weren't even there."

It struck him as odd that there were no real candles in the house. That Shoba hadn't prepared for such an ordinary emergency. He looked now for something to put the birthday candles in and settled on the soil of a potted ivy that normally sat on the windowsill over the sink. Even though the plant was inches from the tap, the soil was so dry that he had to water it first before the candles would stand straight. He pushed aside the things on the kitchen table, the piles of mail, the unread library books. He remembered their first meals there, when they were so thrilled to be married, to be living together in the same house at last, that they would just reach for each other foolishly, more eager to make love than to eat. He put down two embroidered place mats, a wedding gift from an uncle in Lucknow, and set out the plates and wineglasses they usually saved for guests. He put the ivy in the middle, the white-edged, star-shaped leaves girded by ten little candles. He switched on the digital clock radio and tuned it to a jazz station.

"What's all this?" Shoba said when she came downstairs. Her hair was wrapped in a thick white towel. She undid the towel and draped it over a chair, allowing her hair, damp and dark, to fall across her back. As she walked absently toward the stove she took out a few tangles with her fingers. She wore a clean pair of sweatpants, a T-shirt, an old flannel robe. Her stomach was flat again, her waist narrow before the flare of her hips, the belt of the robe tied in a floppy knot.

It was nearly eight. Shukumar put the rice on the table and the lentils from the night before into the microwave oven, punching the numbers on the timer.

"You made *rogan josh*," Shoba observed, looking through the glass lid at the bright paprika stew.

Shukumar took out a piece of lamb, pinching it quickly between his fingers so as not to scald himself. He prodded a larger piece with a serving spoon to make sure the meat slipped easily from the bone. "It's ready," he announced.

The microwave had just beeped when the lights went out, and the music disappeared.

"Perfect timing," Shoba said.

"All I could find were birthday candles." He lit up the ivy, keeping the rest of the candles and a book of matches by his plate.

"It doesn't matter," she said, running a finger along the stem of her wineglass. "It looks lovely."

In the dimness, he knew how she sat, a bit forward in her chair, ankles crossed against the lowest rung, left elbow on the table. During his search for the candles, Shukumar had found a bottle of wine in a crate he had thought was empty. He clamped the bottle between his knees while he turned in the corkscrew. He worried about spilling, and so he picked up the glasses and held them close to his lap while he filled them. They served themselves, stirring the rice with their forks, squinting as they extracted bay leaves and cloves from the stew. Every few minutes Shukumar lit a few more birthday candles and drove them into the soil of the pot.

"It's like India," Shoba said, watching him tend his makeshift candelabra. "Sometimes the current disappears for hours at a stretch. I once had to attend an entire rice ceremony in the dark. The baby just cried and cried. It must have been so hot."

Their baby had never cried, Shukumar considered. Their baby would never have a rice ceremony, even though Shoba had already made the guest list, and decided on which of her three brothers she was going to ask to feed the child its first taste of solid food, at six months if it was a boy, seven if it was a girl.

"Are you hot?" he asked her. He pushed the blazing ivy pot to the other end of the table, closer to the piles of books and mail, making it even more difficult for them to see each other. He was suddenly irritated that he couldn't go upstairs and sit in front of the computer.

"No. It's delicious," she said, tapping her plate with her fork. "It really is."

He refilled the wine in her glass. She thanked him.

They weren't like this before. Now he had to struggle to say something that interested her, something that made her look up from her plate, or from her proofreading files. Eventually he gave up trying to amuse her. He learned not to mind the silences.

"I remember during power failures at my grandmother's house, we all had to say something," Shoba continued. He could barely see her face, but from her tone he knew her eyes were narrowed, as if trying to focus on a distant object. It was a habit of hers.

"Like what?"

"I don't know. A little poem. A joke. A fact about the world. For some reason my relatives always wanted me to tell them the names of my friends in America. I don't know why the information was so interesting to them. The last time I saw my aunt she asked after four girls I went to elementary school with in Tucson. I barely remember them now."

Shukumar hadn't spent as much time in India as Shoba had. His parents, who settled in New Hampshire, used to go back without him. The first time he'd gone as an infant he'd nearly died of amoebic dysentery. His father, a nervous type, was afraid to take him again, in case something were to happen, and left him with his aunt and uncle in Concord. As a teenager he preferred sailing camp or scooping ice cream during the summers to going to Calcutta. It wasn't until after his father died, in his last year of college, that the country began to interest him, and he studied its history from course books as if it were any other subject. He wished now that he had his own childhood story of India.

"Let's do that," she said suddenly.

"Do what?"

"Say something to each other in the dark."

"Like what? I don't know any jokes."

"No, no jokes." She thought for a minute. "How about telling each other something we've never told before."

"I used to play this game in high school," Shukumar recalled. "When I got drunk."

"You're thinking of truth or dare. This is different. Okay, I'll start." She took a sip of wine. "The first time I was alone in your apartment, I looked in your address book to see if you'd written me in. I think we'd known each other two weeks."

"Where was I?"

"You went to answer the telephone in the other room. It was your mother, and I figured it would be a long call. I wanted to know if you'd promoted me from the margins of your newspaper."

"Had I?"

"No. But I didn't give up on you. Now it's your turn."

He couldn't think of anything, but Shoba was waiting for him to speak. She hadn't appeared so determined in months. What was there left to say to her? He thought back to their first meeting, four years earlier at a lecture hall in Cambridge, where a group of Bengali poets were giving a recital. They'd ended up side by side, on folding wooden chairs. Shukumar was soon bored; he was unable to decipher the literary diction, and couldn't join the rest of the audience as they sighed and nodded solemnly after certain phrases. Peering at the newspaper folded in his lap, he studied the temperatures of cities around the world. Ninety-one degrees in Singapore yesterday, fifty-one in Stockholm. When he turned his head to the left, he saw a woman next to him making a grocery list on the back of a folder, and was startled to find that she was beautiful.

"Okay," he said, remembering. "The first time we went out

to dinner, to the Portuguese place, I forgot to tip the waiter. I went back the next morning, found out his name, left money with the manager."

"You went all the way back to Somerville just to tip a waiter?"

"I took a cab."

"Why did you forget to tip the waiter?"

The birthday candles had burned out, but he pictured her face clearly in the dark, the wide tilting eyes, the full grape-toned lips, the fall at age two from her high chair still visible as a comma on her chin. Each day, Shukumar noticed, her beauty, which had once overwhelmed him, seemed to fade. The cosmetics that had seemed superfluous were necessary now, not to improve her but to define her somehow.

"By the end of the meal I had a funny feeling that I might marry you," he said, admitting it to himself as well as to her for the first time. "It must have distracted me."

The next night Shoba came home earlier than usual. There was lamb left over from the evening before, and Shukumar heated it up so that they were able to eat by seven. He'd gone out that day, through the melting snow, and bought a packet of taper candles from the corner store, and batteries to fit the flashlight. He had the candles ready on the countertop, standing in brass holders shaped like lotuses, but they ate under the glow of the copper-shaded ceiling lamp that hung over the table.

When they had finished eating, Shukumar was surprised to see that Shoba was stacking her plate on top of his, and then carrying them over to the sink. He had assumed she would retreat to the living room, behind her barricade of files.

"Don't worry about the dishes," he said, taking them from her hands.

"It seems silly not to," she replied, pouring a drop of detergent onto a sponge. "It's nearly eight o'clock."

His heart quickened. All day Shukumar had looked forward to the lights going out. He thought about what Shoba had said the night before, about looking in his address book. It felt good to remember her as she was then, how bold yet nervous she'd been when they first met, how hopeful. They stood side by side at the sink, their reflections fitting together in the frame of the window. It made him shy, the way he felt the first time they stood together in a mirror. He couldn't recall the last time they'd been photographed. They had stopped attending parties, went nowhere together. The film in his camera still contained pictures of Shoba, in the yard, when she was pregnant.

After finishing the dishes, they leaned against the counter, drying their hands on either end of a towel. At eight o'clock the house went black. Shukumar lit the wicks of the candles, impressed by their long, steady flames.

"Let's sit outside," Shoba said. "I think it's warm still."

They each took a candle and sat down on the steps. It seemed strange to be sitting outside with patches of snow still on the ground. But everyone was out of their houses tonight, the air fresh enough to make people restless. Screen doors opened and closed. A small parade of neighbors passed by with flashlights.

"We're going to the bookstore to browse," a silver-haired man called out. He was walking with his wife, a thin woman in a windbreaker, and holding a dog on a leash. They were the Bradfords, and they had tucked a sympathy card into Shoba and Shukumar's mailbox back in September. "I hear they've got their power."

"They'd better," Shukumar said. "Or you'll be browsing in the dark."

The woman laughed, slipping her arm through the crook of her husband's elbow. "Want to join us?"

"No thanks," Shoba and Shukumar called out together. It surprised Shukumar that his words matched hers.

He wondered what Shoba would tell him in the dark. The worst possibilities had already run through his head. That she'd had an affair. That she didn't respect him for being thirty-five and still a student. That she blamed him for being in Baltimore the way her mother did. But he knew those things weren't true. She'd been faithful, as had he. She believed in him. It was she who had insisted he go to Baltimore. What didn't they know about each other? He knew she curled her fingers tightly when she slept, that her body twitched during bad dreams. He knew it was honeydew she favored over cantaloupe. He knew that when they returned from the hospital the first thing she did when she walked into the house was pick out objects of theirs and toss them into a pile in the hallway: books from the shelves, plants from the windowsills, paintings from walls, photos from tables, pots and pans that hung from the hooks over the stove. Shukumar had stepped out of her way, watching as she moved methodically from room to room. When she was satisfied, she stood there staring at the pile she'd made, her lips drawn back in such distaste that Shukumar had thought she would spit. Then she'd started to cry.

He began to feel cold as he sat there on the steps. He felt that he needed her to talk first, in order to reciprocate.

"That time when your mother came to visit us," she said finally. "When I said one night that I had to stay late at work, I went out with Gillian and had a martini."

He looked at her profile, the slender nose, the slightly masculine set of her jaw. He remembered that night well; eating with his mother, tired from teaching two classes back to back, wishing Shoba were there to say more of the right things because he came up with only the wrong ones. It had been twelve years since his father had died, and his mother had come to spend two weeks with him and Shoba, so they could honor his father's memory together. Each night his mother cooked something his father had liked, but she was too upset to eat the dishes herself, and her eyes would well up as Shoba stroked her hand. "It's so touching," Shoba had said to him at the time. Now he pictured Shoba with Gillian, in a bar with striped velvet sofas, the one they used to go to after the movies, making sure she got her extra olive, asking Gillian for a cigarette. He imagined her complaining, and Gillian sympathizing about visits from in-laws. It was Gillian who had driven Shoba to the hospital.

"Your turn," she said, stopping his thoughts.

At the end of their street Shukumar heard sounds of a drill and the electricians shouting over it. He looked at the darkened facades of the houses lining the street. Candles glowed in the windows of one. In spite of the warmth, smoke rose from the chimney.

"I cheated on my Oriental Civilization exam in college," he said. "It was my last semester, my last set of exams. My father had died a few months before. I could see the blue book of the guy next to me. He was an American guy, a maniac. He knew Urdu and Sanskrit. I couldn't remember if the verse we had to identify was an example of a *ghazal* or not. I looked at his answer and copied it down."

It had happened over fifteen years ago. He felt relief now, having told her.

She turned to him, looking not at his face, but at his shoes — old moccasins he wore as if they were slippers, the leather at the back permanently flattened. He wondered if it bothered her, what he'd said. She took his hand and pressed it. "You didn't have to tell me why you did it," she said, moving closer to him.

They sat together until nine o'clock, when the lights came on. They heard some people across the street clapping from their porch, and televisions being turned on. The Bradfords walked back down the street, eating ice-cream cones and waving. Shoba and Shukumar waved back. Then they stood up, his hand still in hers, and went inside.

Somehow, without saying anything, it had turned into this. Into an exchange of confessions — the little ways they'd hurt or disappointed each other, and themselves. The following day Shukumar thought for hours about what to say to her. He was torn between admitting that he once ripped out a photo of a woman in one of the fashion magazines she used to subscribe to and carried it in his books for a week, or saying that he really hadn't lost the sweater-vest she bought him for their third wedding anniversary but had exchanged it for cash at Filene's, and that he had gotten drunk alone in the middle of the day at a hotel bar. For their first anniversary, Shoba had cooked a ten-course dinner just for him. The vest depressed him. "My wife gave me a sweater-vest for our anniversary," he complained to the bartender, his head heavy with cognac. "What do you expect?" the bartender had replied. "You're married."

As for the picture of the woman, he didn't know why he'd ripped it out. She wasn't as pretty as Shoba. She wore a white sequined dress, and had a sullen face and lean, mannish legs. Her bare arms were raised, her fists around her head, as if she were about to punch herself in the ears. It was an advertisement for stockings. Shoba had been pregnant at the time, her stomach suddenly immense, to the point where Shukumar no longer wanted to touch her. The first time he saw the picture he was lying in bed next to her, watching her as she read. When he noticed the magazine in the recycling pile he found the woman and tore out the page as carefully as he could. For about a week he allowed himself a glimpse each day. He felt an intense desire for the woman, but it was a desire that turned to disgust after a minute or two. It was the closest he'd come to infidelity.

He told Shoba about the sweater on the third night, the picture on the fourth. She said nothing as he spoke, expressed no protest or reproach. She simply listened, and then she took his hand, pressing it as she had before. On the third night, she told him that once after a lecture they'd attended, she let him speak to the chairman of his department without telling him that he had a dab of pâté on his chin. She'd been irritated with him for some reason, and so she'd let him go on and on, about securing his fellowship for the following semester, without putting a finger to her own chin as a signal. The fourth night, she said that she never liked the one poem he'd ever published in his life, in a literary magazine in Utah. He'd written the poem after meeting Shoba. She added that she found the poem sentimental.

Something happened when the house was dark. They were able to talk to each other again. The third night after supper they'd sat together on the sofa, and once it was dark he began kissing her awkwardly on her forehead and her face, and though it was dark he closed his eyes, and knew that she did, too. The fourth night they walked carefully upstairs, to bed, feeling together for the final step with their feet before the landing, and making love with a desperation they had forgotten. She wept without sound, and whispered his name, and traced his eyebrows with her finger in the dark. As he made love to her he wondered what he would say to her the next night, and what she would say, the thought of it exciting him. "Hold me," he said, "hold me in your arms." By the time the lights came back on downstairs, they'd fallen asleep.

The morning of the fifth night Shukumar found another notice from the electric company in the mailbox. The line had been repaired ahead of schedule, it said. He was disappointed. He had planned on making shrimp *malai* for Shoba, but when he arrived at the store he didn't feel like cooking anymore. It wasn't the same, he thought, knowing that the lights wouldn't go out. In the store the shrimp looked gray and thin. The coconut milk tin was dusty and overpriced. Still, he bought them, along with a beeswax candle and two bottles of wine.

She came home at seven-thirty. "I suppose this is the end of our game," he said when he saw her reading the notice.

She looked at him. "You can still light candles if you want." She hadn't been to the gym tonight. She wore a suit beneath the raincoat. Her makeup had been retouched recently.

When she went upstairs to change, Shukumar poured himself some wine and put on a record, a Thelonius Monk album he knew she liked.

When she came downstairs they ate together. She didn't thank him or compliment him. They simply ate in a darkened room, in the glow of a beeswax candle. They had survived a difficult time. They finished off the shrimp. They finished off the first bottle of wine and moved on to the second. They sat together until the candle had nearly burned away. She shifted in her chair, and Shukumar thought that she was about to say something. But instead she blew out the candle, stood up, turned on the light switch, and sat down again.

"Shouldn't we keep the lights off?" Shukumar asked.

She set her plate aside and clasped her hands on the table. "I want you to see my face when I tell you this," she said gently.

His heart began to pound. The day she told him she was pregnant, she had used the very same words, saying them in the same gentle way, turning off the basketball game he'd been watching on television. He hadn't been prepared then. Now he was.

Only he didn't want her to be pregnant again. He didn't want to have to pretend to be happy.

"I've been looking for an apartment and I've found one," she said, narrowing her eyes on something, it seemed, behind his left shoulder. It was nobody's fault, she continued. They'd been through enough. She needed some time alone. She had money saved up for a security deposit. The apartment was on Beacon Hill, so she could walk to work. She had signed the lease that night before coming home.

She wouldn't look at him, but he stared at her. It was obvious that she'd rehearsed the lines. All this time she'd been looking for an apartment, testing the water pressure, asking a Realtor if heat and hot water were included in the rent. It sickened Shukumar, knowing that she had spent these past evenings preparing for a life without him. He was relieved and yet he was sickened. This was what she'd been trying to tell him for the past four evenings. This was the point of her game.

Now it was his turn to speak. There was something he'd sworn he would never tell her, and for six months he had done his best to block it from his mind. Before the ultrasound she had asked the doctor not to tell her the sex of their child, and Shukumar had agreed. She had wanted it to be a surprise.

Later, those few times they talked about what had happened, she said at least they'd been spared that knowledge. In a way she almost took pride in her decision, for it enabled her to seek refuge in a mystery. He knew that she assumed it was a

mystery for him, too. He'd arrived too late from Baltimore —
when it was all over and she was lying on the hospital bed. But
he hadn't. He'd arrived early enough to see their baby, and to
hold him before they cremated him. At first he had recoiled at
the suggestion, but the doctor said holding the baby might
help him with the process of grieving. Shoba was asleep. The
baby had been cleaned off, his bulbous lids shut tight to the
world.

"Our baby was a boy," he said. "His skin was more red than
brown. He had black hair on his head. He weighed almost five
pounds. His fingers were curled shut, just like yours in the
night."

Shoba looked at him now, her face contorted with sor-
row. He had cheated on a college exam, ripped a picture of a
woman out of a magazine. He had returned a sweater and got
drunk in the middle of the day instead. These were the things
he had told her. He had held his son, who had known life
only within her, against his chest in a darkened room in an
unknown wing of the hospital. He had held him until a nurse
knocked and took him away, and he promised himself that day
that he would never tell Shoba, because he still loved her then,
and it was the one thing in her life that she had wanted to be a
surprise.

Shukumar stood up and stacked his plate on top of hers. He
carried the plates to the sink, but instead of running the tap he
looked out the window. Outside the evening was still warm,
and the Bradfords were walking arm in arm. As he watched
the couple the room went dark, and he spun around. Shoba
had turned the lights off. She came back to the table and sat
down, and after a moment Shukumar joined her. They wept
together, for the things they now knew.

When Mr. Pirzada Came to Dine

IN THE AUTUMN OF 1971 a man used to come to our house, bearing confections in his pocket and hopes of ascertaining the life or death of his family. His name was Mr. Pirzada, and he came from Dacca, now the capital of Bangladesh, but then a part of Pakistan. That year Pakistan was engaged in civil war. The eastern frontier, where Dacca was located, was fighting for autonomy from the ruling regime in the west. In March, Dacca had been invaded, torched, and shelled by the Pakistani army. Teachers were dragged onto streets and shot, women dragged into barracks and raped. By the end of the summer, three hundred thousand people were said to have died. In Dacca Mr. Pirzada had a three-story home, a lectureship in botany at the university, a wife of twenty years, and seven daughters between the ages of six and sixteen whose names all began with the letter A. "Their mother's idea," he explained one day, producing from his wallet a black-and-white picture of seven girls at a picnic, their braids tied with ribbons, sitting cross-legged in a row, eating chicken curry off of banana leaves. "How am I to distinguish? Ayesha, Amira, Amina, Aziza, you see the difficulty."

Each week Mr. Pirzada wrote letters to his wife, and sent comic books to each of his seven daughters, but the postal system, along with most everything else in Dacca, had collapsed, and he had not heard word of them in over six months. Mr. Pirzada, meanwhile, was in America for the year, for he had been awarded a grant from the government of Pakistan to study the foliage of New England. In spring and summer he had gathered data in Vermont and Maine, and in autumn he moved to a university north of Boston, where we lived, to write a short book about his discoveries. The grant was a great honor, but when converted into dollars it was not generous. As a result, Mr. Pirzada lived in a room in a graduate dormitory, and did not own a proper stove or a television set of his own. And so he came to our house to eat dinner and watch the evening news.

At first I knew nothing of the reason for his visits. I was ten years old, and was not surprised that my parents, who were from India, and had a number of Indian acquaintances at the university, should ask Mr. Pirzada to share our meals. It was a small campus, with narrow brick walkways and white pillared buildings, located on the fringes of what seemed to be an even smaller town. The supermarket did not carry mustard oil, doctors did not make house calls, neighbors never dropped by without an invitation, and of these things, every so often, my parents complained. In search of compatriots, they used to trail their fingers, at the start of each new semester, through the columns of the university directory, circling surnames familiar to their part of the world. It was in this manner that they discovered Mr. Pirzada, and phoned him, and invited him to our home.

I have no memory of his first visit, or of his second or his third, but by the end of September I had grown so accustomed to Mr. Pirzada's presence in our living room that one evening, as I was dropping ice cubes into the water pitcher, I asked my mother to hand me a fourth glass from a cupboard still out of my reach. She was busy at the stove, presiding over a skillet of fried spinach with radishes, and could not hear me because of the drone of the exhaust fan and the fierce scrapes of her spatula. I turned to my father, who was leaning against the refrigerator, eating spiced cashews from a cupped fist.

"What is it, Lilia?"

"A glass for the Indian man."

"Mr. Pirzada won't be coming today. More importantly, Mr. Pirzada is no longer considered Indian," my father announced, brushing salt from the cashews out of his trim black beard. "Not since Partition. Our country was divided. 1947."

When I said I thought that was the date of India's independence from Britain, my father said, "That too. One moment we were free and then we were sliced up," he explained, drawing an X with his finger on the countertop, "like a pie. Hindus here, Muslims there. Dacca no longer belongs to us." He told me that during Partition Hindus and Muslims had set fire to each other's homes. For many, the idea of eating in the other's company was still unthinkable.

It made no sense to me. Mr. Pirzada and my parents spoke the same language, laughed at the same jokes, looked more or less the same. They ate pickled mangoes with their meals, ate rice every night for supper with their hands. Like my parents, Mr. Pirzada took off his shoes before entering a room, chewed fennel seeds after meals as a digestive, drank no alcohol, for dessert dipped austere biscuits into successive cups of tea. Nevertheless my father insisted that I understand the difference, and he led me to a map of the world taped to the wall over his desk. He seemed concerned that Mr. Pirzada might take offense if I accidentally referred to him as an Indian, though I could not really imagine Mr. Pirzada being offended by much of anything. "Mr. Pirzada is Bengali, but he is a Muslim," my father informed me. "Therefore he lives in East Pakistan, not India." His finger trailed across the Atlantic, through Europe, the Mediterranean, the Middle East, and finally to the sprawling orange diamond that my mother once told me resembled a woman wearing a sari with her left arm extended. Various cities had been circled with lines drawn between them to indicate my parents' travels, and the place of their birth, Calcutta, was signified by a small silver star. I had been there only once and had no memory of the trip. "As you see, Lilia, it is a different country, a different color," my father said. Pakistan was yellow, not orange. I noticed that there were two distinct parts to it, one much larger than the other, separated by an expanse of Indian territory; it was as if California and Connecticut constituted a nation apart from the U.S.

My father rapped his knuckles on top of my head. "You are, of course, aware of the current situation? Aware of East Pakistan's fight for sovereignty?"

I nodded, unaware of the situation.

We returned to the kitchen, where my mother was draining a pot of boiled rice into a colander. My father opened up the can on the counter and eyed me sharply over the frames of his glasses as he ate some more cashews. "What exactly do they teach you at school? Do you study history? Geography?"

"Lilia has plenty to learn at school," my mother said. "We live here now, she was born here." She seemed genuinely proud of the fact, as if it were a reflection of my character. In her estimation, I knew, I was assured a safe life, an easy life, a fine education, every opportunity. I would never have to eat rationed food, or obey curfews, or watch riots from my rooftop, or hide neighbors in water tanks to prevent them from being shot, as she and my father had. "Imagine having to place her in a decent school. Imagine her having to read during power failures by the light of kerosene lamps. Imagine the pressures, the tutors, the constant exams." She ran a hand through her hair, bobbed to a suitable length for her part-time job as a bank teller. "How can you possibly expect her to know about Partition? Put those nuts away."

"But what does she learn about the world?" My father rattled the cashew can in his hand. "What is she learning?"

We learned American history, of course, and American geography. That year, and every year, it seemed, we began by studying the Revolutionary War. We were taken in school buses on field trips to visit Plymouth Rock, and to walk the Freedom Trail, and to climb to the top of the Bunker Hill Monument. We made dioramas out of colored construction paper depicting George Washington crossing the choppy waters of the Delaware River, and we made puppets of King George wearing white tights and a black bow in his hair. During tests we were given blank maps of the thirteen colonies, and asked to fill in names, dates, capitals. I could do it with my eyes closed.

The next evening Mr. Pirzada arrived, as usual, at six o'clock. Though they were no longer strangers, upon first greeting each other, he and my father maintained the habit of shaking hands.

"Come in, sir. Lilia, Mr. Pirzada's coat, please."

He stepped into the foyer, impeccably suited and scarved, with a silk tie knotted at his collar. Each evening he appeared in ensembles of plums, olives, and chocolate browns. He was a compact man, and though his feet were perpetually splayed, and his belly slightly wide, he nevertheless maintained an efficient posture, as if balancing in either hand two suitcases of equal weight. His ears were insulated by tufts of graying hair that seemed to block out the unpleasant traffic of life. He had thickly lashed eyes shaded with a trace of camphor, a generous mustache that turned up playfully at the ends, and a mole shaped like a flattened raisin in the very center of his left cheek. On his head he wore a black fez made from the wool of Persian lambs, secured by bobby pins, without which I was never to see him. Though my father always offered to fetch him in our car, Mr. Pirzada preferred to walk from his dormitory to our neighborhood, a distance of about twenty minutes on foot, studying trees and shrubs on his way, and when he entered our house his knuckles were pink with the effects of crisp autumn air.

"Another refugee, I am afraid, on Indian territory."

"They are estimating nine million at the last count," my father said.

Mr. Pirzada handed me his coat, for it was my job to hang it on the rack at the bottom of the stairs. It was made of finely checkered gray-and-blue wool, with a striped lining and horn buttons, and carried in its weave the faint smell of limes. There were no recognizable tags inside, only a hand-stitched label with the phrase "Z. Sayeed, Suitors" embroidered on it in cursive with glossy black thread. On certain days a birch or maple leaf was tucked into a pocket. He unlaced his shoes and lined them against the baseboard; a golden paste clung to the toes and heels, the result of walking through our damp, unraked lawn. Relieved of his trappings, he grazed my throat with his short, restless fingers, the way a person feels for solidity behind a wall before driving in a nail. Then he followed my father to the living room, where the television was tuned to the local news. As soon as they were seated my mother appeared from the kitchen with a plate of mincemeat kebabs with coriander chutney. Mr. Pirzada popped one into his mouth.

"One can only hope," he said, reaching for another, "that Dacca's refugees are as heartily fed. Which reminds me." He reached into his suit pocket and gave me a small plastic egg filled with cinnamon hearts. "For the lady of the house," he said with an almost imperceptible splay-footed bow.

"Really, Mr. Pirzada," my mother protested. "Night after night. You spoil her."

"I only spoil children who are incapable of spoiling."

It was an awkward moment for me, one which I awaited in part with dread, in part with delight. I was charmed by the presence of Mr. Pirzada's rotund elegance, and flattered by the faint theatricality of his attentions, yet unsettled by the superb ease of his gestures, which made me feel, for an instant, like a stranger in my own home. It had become our ritual, and for several weeks, before we grew more comfortable with one another, it was the only time he spoke to me directly. I had no response, offered no comment, betrayed no visible reaction to the steady stream of honey-filled lozenges, the raspberry truffles, the slender rolls of sour pastilles. I could not even thank him, for once, when I did, for an especially spectacular peppermint lollipop wrapped in a spray of purple cellophane, he had demanded, "What is this thank-you? The lady at the bank thanks me, the cashier at the shop thanks me, the librarian thanks me when I return an overdue book, the overseas operator thanks me as she tries to connect me to Dacca and fails. If I am buried in this country I will be thanked, no doubt, at my funeral."

It was inappropriate, in my opinion, to consume the candy Mr. Pirzada gave me in a casual manner. I coveted each evening's treasure as I would a jewel, or a coin from a buried kingdom, and I would place it in a small keepsake box made of carved sandalwood beside my bed, in which, long ago in India, my father's mother used to store the ground areca nuts she ate after her morning bath. It was my only memento of a grand-mother I had never known, and until Mr. Pirzada came to our lives I could find nothing to put inside it. Every so often before brushing my teeth and laying out my clothes for school the next day, I opened the lid of the box and ate one of his treats.

That night, like every night, we did not eat at the dining table, because it did not provide an unobstructed view of the television set. Instead we huddled around the coffee table, without conversing, our plates perched on the edges of our knees. From the kitchen my mother brought forth the succession of dishes: lentils with fried onions, green beans with coconut, fish cooked with raisins in a yogurt sauce. I followed with the water glasses, and the plate of lemon wedges, and the chili peppers, purchased on monthly trips to Chinatown and stored by the pound in the freezer, which they liked to snap open and crush into their food.

Before eating Mr. Pirzada always did a curious thing. He took out a plain silver watch without a band, which he kept in his breast pocket, held it briefly to one of his tufted ears, and wound it with three swift flicks of his thumb and forefinger. Unlike the watch on his wrist, the pocket watch, he had explained to me, was set to the local time in Dacca, eleven hours ahead. For the duration of the meal the watch rested on his folded paper napkin on the coffee table. He never seemed to consult it.

Now that I had learned Mr. Pirzada was not an Indian, I began to study him with extra care, to try to figure out what made him different. I decided that the pocket watch was one of those things. When I saw it that night, as he wound it and arranged it on the coffee table, an uneasiness possessed me; life, I realized, was being lived in Dacca first. I imagined Mr. Pirzada's daughters rising from sleep, tying ribbons in their hair, anticipating breakfast, preparing for school. Our meals, our actions, were only a shadow of what had already happened there, a lagging ghost of where Mr. Pirzada really belonged.

At six-thirty, which was when the national news began, my father raised the volume and adjusted the antennas. Usually I occupied myself with a book, but that night my father insisted that I pay attention. On the screen I saw tanks rolling through dusty streets, and fallen buildings, and forests of unfamiliar trees into which East Pakistani refugees had fled, seeking safety over the Indian border. I saw boats with fan-shaped sails floating on wide coffee-colored rivers, a barricaded university, newspaper offices burnt to the ground. I turned to look at Mr. Pirzada; the images flashed in miniature across his eyes. As he watched he had an immovable expression on his face, composed but alert, as if someone were giving him directions to an unknown destination.

During the commercial my mother went to the kitchen to get more rice, and my father and Mr. Pirzada deplored the policies of a general named Yahyah Khan. They discussed intrigues I did not know, a catastrophe I could not comprehend. "See, children your age, what they do to survive," my father said as he served me another piece of fish. But I could no longer eat. I could only steal glances at Mr. Pirzada, sitting beside me in his olive green jacket, calmly creating a well in his rice to make room for a second helping of lentils. He was not my notion of a man burdened by such grave concerns. I wondered if the reason he was always so smartly dressed was in preparation to endure with dignity whatever news assailed him, perhaps even to attend a funeral at a moment's notice. I wondered, too, what would happen if suddenly his seven daughters were to appear on television, smiling and waving and blowing kisses to Mr. Pirzada from a balcony. I imagined how relieved he would be. But this never happened.

That night when I placed the plastic egg filled with cinnamon hearts in the box beside my bed, I did not feel the ceremonious satisfaction I normally did. I tried not to think about Mr. Pirzada, in his lime-scented overcoat, connected to the unruly, sweltering world we had viewed a few hours ago in our bright, carpeted living room. And yet for several moments that was all I could think about. My stomach tightened as I worried whether his wife and seven daughters were now members of the drifting, clamoring crowd that had flashed at intervals on the screen. In an effort to banish the image I looked around my room, at the yellow canopied bed with matching flounced curtains, at framed class pictures mounted on white and violet papered walls, at the penciled inscriptions by the closet door where my father recorded my height on each of my birthdays. But the more I tried to distract myself, the more I began to convince myself that Mr. Pirzada's family was in all likelihood dead. Eventually I took a square of white chocolate out of the box, and unwrapped it, and then I did something I had never done before. I put the chocolate in my mouth, letting it soften until the last possible moment, and then as I chewed it slowly, I prayed that Mr. Pirzada's family was safe and sound. I had never prayed for anything before, had never been taught or told to, but I decided, given the circumstances, that it was something I should do. That night when I went to the bathroom I only pretended to brush my teeth, for I feared that I would somehow rinse the prayer out as well. I wet the brush and rearranged the tube of paste to prevent my parents from asking any questions, and fell asleep with sugar on my tongue.

No one at school talked about the war followed so faithfully in my living room. We continued to study the American Revolution, and learned about the injustices of taxation without representation, and memorized passages from the Declaration of Independence. During recess the boys would divide in two groups, chasing each other wildly around the swings and seesaws, Redcoats against the colonies. In the classroom our teacher, Mrs. Kenyon, pointed frequently to a map that emerged like a movie screen from the top of the chalkboard, charting the route of the *Mayflower,* or showing us the location of the Liberty Bell. Each week two members of the class gave a report on a particular aspect of the Revolution, and so one day I was sent to the school library with my friend Dora to learn about the surrender at Yorktown. Mrs. Kenyon handed us a slip of paper with the names of three books to look up in the card catalogue. We found them right away, and sat down at a low round table to read and take notes. But I could not concentrate. I returned to the blond-wood shelves, to a section I had noticed labeled "Asia." I saw books about China, India, Indonesia, Korea. Eventually I found a book titled *Pakistan: A Land and Its People.* I sat on a footstool and opened the book. The laminated jacket crackled in my grip. I began turning the pages, filled with photos of rivers and rice fields and men in military uniforms. There was a chapter about Dacca, and I began to read about its rainfall, and its jute production. I was studying a population chart when Dora appeared in the aisle.

"What are you doing back here? Mrs. Kenyon's in the library. She came to check up on us."

I slammed the book shut, too loudly. Mrs. Kenyon emerged, the aroma of her perfume filling up the tiny aisle, and lifted the book by the tip of its spine as if it were a hair clinging to my sweater. She glanced at the cover, then at me.

"Is this book a part of your report, Lilia?"

"No, Mrs. Kenyon."

"Then I see no reason to consult it," she said, replacing it in the slim gap on the shelf. "Do you?"

* * *

As weeks passed it grew more and more rare to see any footage from Dacca on the news. The report came after the first set of commercials, sometimes the second. The press had been censored, removed, restricted, rerouted. Some days, many days, only a death toll was announced, prefaced by a reiteration of the general situation. More poets were executed, more villages set ablaze. In spite of it all, night after night, my parents and Mr. Pirzada enjoyed long, leisurely meals. After the television was shut off, and the dishes washed and dried, they joked, and told stories, and dipped biscuits in their tea. When they tired of discussing political matters they discussed, instead, the progress of Mr. Pirzada's book about the deciduous trees of New England, and my father's nomination for tenure, and the peculiar eating habits of my mother's American coworkers at the bank. Eventually I was sent upstairs to do my homework, but through the carpet I heard them as they drank more tea, and listened to cassettes of Kishore Kumar, and played Scrabble on the coffee table, laughing and arguing long into the night about the spellings of English words. I wanted to join them, wanted, above all, to console Mr. Pirzada somehow. But apart from eating a piece of candy for the sake of his family and praying for their safety, there was nothing I could do. They played Scrabble until the eleven o'clock news, and then, sometime around midnight, Mr. Pirzada walked back to his dormitory. For this reason I never saw him leave, but each night as I drifted off to sleep I would hear them, anticipating the birth of a nation on the other side of the world.

One day in October Mr. Pirzada asked upon arrival, "What are these large orange vegetables on people's doorsteps? A type of squash?"

"Pumpkins," my mother replied. "Lilia, remind me to pick one up at the supermarket."

"And the purpose? It indicates what?"

"You make a jack-o'-lantern," I said, grinning ferociously. "Like this. To scare people away."

"I see," Mr. Pirzada said, grinning back. "Very useful."

The next day my mother bought a ten-pound pumpkin, fat and round, and placed it on the dining table. Before supper, while my father and Mr. Pirzada were watching the local news, she told me to decorate it with markers, but I wanted to carve it properly like others I had noticed in the neighborhood.

"Yes, let's carve it," Mr. Pirzada agreed, and rose from the sofa. "Hang the news tonight." Asking no questions, he walked into the kitchen, opened a drawer, and returned, bearing a long serrated knife. He glanced at me for approval. "Shall I?"

I nodded. For the first time we all gathered around the dining table, my mother, my father, Mr. Pirzada, and I. While the television aired unattended we covered the tabletop with newspapers. Mr. Pirzada draped his jacket over the chair behind him, removed a pair of opal cuff links, and rolled up the starched sleeves of his shirt.

"First go around the top, like this," I instructed, demonstrating with my index finger.

He made an initial incision and drew the knife around. When he had come full circle he lifted the cap by the stem; it loosened effortlessly, and Mr. Pirzada leaned over the pumpkin for a moment to inspect and inhale its contents. My mother gave him a long metal spoon with which he gutted the interior until the last bits of string and seeds were gone. My father, meanwhile, separated the seeds from the pulp and set them out to dry on a cookie sheet, so that we could roast them later on. I drew two triangles against the ridged surface for the

eyes, which Mr. Pirzada dutifully carved, and crescents for eyebrows, and another triangle for the nose. The mouth was all
that remained, and the teeth posed a challenge. I hesitated.

"Smile or frown?" I asked.

"You choose," Mr. Pirzada said.

As a compromise I drew a kind of grimace, straight across,
neither mournful nor friendly. Mr. Pirzada began carving,
without the least bit of intimidation, as if he had been carving
jack-o'-lanterns his whole life. He had nearly finished when the
national news began. The reporter mentioned Dacca, and we
all turned to listen: An Indian official announced that unless
the world helped to relieve the burden of East Pakistani refugees, India would have to go to war against Pakistan. The
reporter's face dripped with sweat as he relayed the information. He did not wear a tie or a jacket, dressed instead as if he
himself were about to take part in the battle. He shielded his
scorched face as he hollered things to the cameraman. The
knife slipped from Mr. Pirzada's hand and made a gash dipping
toward the base of the pumpkin.

"Please forgive me." He raised a hand to one side of his face,
as if someone had slapped him there. "I am — it is terrible. I
will buy another. We will try again."

"Not at all, not at all," my father said. He took the knife
from Mr. Pirzada, and carved around the gash, evening it out,
dispensing altogether with the teeth I had drawn. What re-
sulted was a disproportionately large hole the size of a lemon,
so that our jack-o'-lantern wore an expression of placid astonishment, the eyebrows no longer fierce, floating in frozen surprise above a vacant, geometric gaze.

For Halloween I was a witch. Dora, my trick-or-treating part-
ner, was a witch too. We wore black capes fashioned from

dyed pillowcases and conical hats with wide cardboard brims. We shaded our faces green with a broken eye shadow that belonged to Dora's mother, and my mother gave us two burlap sacks that had once contained basmati rice, for collecting candy. That year our parents decided that we were old enough to roam the neighborhood unattended. Our plan was to walk from my house to Dora's, from where I was to call to say I had arrived safely, and then Dora's mother would drive me home. My father equipped us with flashlights, and I had to wear my watch and synchronize it with his. We were to return no later than nine o'clock.

When Mr. Pirzada arrived that evening he presented me with a box of chocolate-covered mints.

"In here," I told him, and opened up the burlap sack. "Trick or treat!"

"I understand that you don't really need my contribution this evening," he said, depositing the box. He gazed at my green face, and the hat secured by a string under my chin. Gingerly he lifted the hem of the cape, under which I was wearing a sweater and a zipped fleece jacket. "Will you be warm enough?"

I nodded, causing the hat to tip to one side.

He set it right. "Perhaps it is best to stand still."

The bottom of our staircase was lined with baskets of miniature candy, and when Mr. Pirzada removed his shoes he did not place them there as he normally did, but inside the closet instead. He began to unbutton his coat, and I waited to take it from him, but Dora called me from the bathroom to say that she needed my help drawing a mole on her chin. When we were finally ready my mother took a picture of us in front of the fireplace, and then I opened the front door to leave. Mr. Pirzada and my father, who had not gone into the living room yet, hovered in the foyer. Outside it was already dark. The air smelled of wet leaves, and our carved jack-o'-lantern flickered impressively against the shrubbery by the door. In the distance came the sounds of scampering feet, and the howls of the older boys who wore no costume at all other than a rubber mask, and the rustling apparel of the youngest children, some so young that they were carried from door to door in the arms of their parents.

"Don't go into any of the houses you don't know," my father warned.

Mr. Pirzada knit his brows together. "Is there any danger?"

"No, no," my mother assured him. "All the children will be out. It's a tradition."

"Perhaps I should accompany them?" Mr. Pirzada suggested. He looked suddenly tired and small, standing there in his splayed, stockinged feet, and his eyes contained a panic I had never seen before. In spite of the cold I began to sweat inside my pillowcase.

"Really, Mr. Pirzada," my mother said, "Lilia will be perfectly safe with her friend."

"But if it rains? If they lose their way?"

"Don't worry," I said. It was the first time I had uttered those words to Mr. Pirzada, two simple words I had tried but failed to tell him for weeks, had said only in my prayers. It shamed me now that I had said them for my own sake.

He placed one of his stocky fingers on my cheek, then pressed it to the back of his own hand, leaving a faint green smear. "If the lady insists," he conceded, and offered a small bow.

We left, stumbling slightly in our black pointy thrift-store shoes, and when we turned at the end of the driveway to wave good-bye, Mr. Pirzada was standing in the frame of the doorway, a short figure between my parents, waving back.

"Why did that man want to come with us?" Dora asked.

"His daughters are missing." As soon as I said it, I wished I had not. I felt that my saying it made it true, that Mr. Pirzada's daughters really were missing, and that he would never see them again.

"You mean they were kidnapped?" Dora continued. "From a park or something?"

"I didn't mean they were missing. I meant, he misses them. They live in a different country, and he hasn't seen them in a while, that's all."

We went from house to house, walking along pathways and pressing doorbells. Some people had switched off all their lights for effect, or strung rubber bats in their windows. At the McIntyres' a coffin was placed in front of the door, and Mr. McIntyre rose from it in silence, his face covered with chalk, and deposited a fistful of candy corns into our sacks. Several people told me that they had never seen an Indian witch before. Others performed the transaction without comment. As we paved our way with the parallel beams of our flashlights we saw eggs cracked in the middle of the road, and cars covered with shaving cream, and toilet paper garlanding the branches of trees. By the time we reached Dora's house our hands were chapped from carrying our bulging burlap bags, and our feet were sore and swollen. Her mother gave us bandages for our blisters and served us warm cider and caramel popcorn. She reminded me to call my parents to tell them I had arrived safely, and when I did I could hear the television in the background. My mother did not seem particularly relieved to hear from me. When I replaced the phone on the receiver it occurred to me that the television wasn't on at Dora's house at all. Her father was lying on the couch, reading a magazine, with a glass of wine on the coffee table, and there was saxophone music playing on the stereo.

After Dora and I had sorted through our plunder, and counted and sampled and traded until we were satisfied, her mother drove me back to my house. I thanked her for the ride, and she waited in the driveway until I made it to the door. In the glare of her headlights I saw that our pumpkin had been shattered, its thick shell strewn in chunks across the grass. I felt the sting of tears in my eyes, and a sudden pain in my throat, as if it had been stuffed with the sharp tiny pebbles that crunched with each step under my aching feet. I opened the door, expecting the three of them to be standing in the foyer, waiting to receive me, and to grieve for our ruined pumpkin, but there was no one. In the living room Mr. Pirzada, my father, and mother were sitting side by side on the sofa. The television was turned off, and Mr. Pirzada had his head in his hands.

What they heard that evening, and for many evenings after that, was that India and Pakistan were drawing closer and closer to war. Troops from both sides lined the border, and Dacca was insisting on nothing short of independence. The war was to be waged on East Pakistani soil. The United States was siding with West Pakistan, the Soviet Union with India and what was soon to be Bangladesh. War was declared officially on December 4, and twelve days later, the Pakistani army, weakened by having to fight three thousand miles from their source of supplies, surrendered in Dacca. All of these facts I know only now, for they are available to me in any history book, in any library. But then it remained, for the most part, a remote mystery with haphazard clues. What I remember during those twelve days of the war was that my father no longer asked me to watch the news with them, and that Mr. Pirzada stopped bringing me candy, and that my mother refused to serve anything other than boiled eggs with rice for dinner. I remember some nights helping my mother spread a sheet and blankets on the couch so that Mr. Pirzada could sleep there, and high-pitched voices hollering in the middle of the night when my parents called our relatives in Calcutta to learn more details about the situation. Most of all I remember the three of them operating during that time as if they were a single person, sharing a single meal, a single body, a single silence, and a single fear.

In January, Mr. Pirzada flew back to his three-story home in Dacca, to discover what was left of it. We did not see much of him in those final weeks of the year; he was busy finishing his manuscript, and we went to Philadelphia to spend Christmas with friends of my parents. Just as I have no memory of his first visit, I have no memory of his last. My father drove him to the airport one afternoon while I was at school. For a long time we did not hear from him. Our evenings went on as usual, with dinners in front of the news. The only difference was that Mr. Pirzada and his extra watch were not there to accompany us. According to reports Dacca was repairing itself slowly, with a newly formed parliamentary government. The new leader, Sheikh Mujib Rahman, recently released from prison, asked countries for building materials to replace more than one million houses that had been destroyed in the war. Countless refugees returned from India, greeted, we learned, by unemployment and the threat of famine. Every now and then I studied the map above my father's desk and pictured Mr. Pirzada on that small patch of yellow, perspiring heavily, I imagined, in one of his suits, searching for his family. Of course, the map was outdated by then.

Finally, several months later, we received a card from Mr. Pirzada commemorating the Muslim New Year, along with a short letter. He was reunited, he wrote, with his wife and children. All were well, having survived the events of the past year at an estate belonging to his wife's grandparents in the mountains of Shillong. His seven daughters were a bit taller, he wrote, but otherwise they were the same, and he still could not keep their names in order. At the end of the letter he thanked us for our hospitality, adding that although he now understood the meaning of the words "thank you" they still were not adequate to express his gratitude. To celebrate the good news my mother prepared a special dinner that evening, and when we sat down to eat at the coffee table we toasted our water glasses, but I did not feel like celebrating. Though I had not seen him for months, it was only then that I felt Mr. Pirzada's absence. It was only then, raising my water glass in his name, that I knew what it meant to miss someone who was so many miles and hours away, just as he had missed his wife and daughters for so many months. He had no reason to return to us, and my parents predicted, correctly, that we would never see him again. Since January, each night before bed, I had continued to eat, for the sake of Mr. Pirzada's family, a piece of candy I had saved from Halloween. That night there was no need to. Eventually, I threw them away.

Interpreter of Maladies

A T THE TEA STALL Mr. and Mrs. Das bickered about who should take Tina to the toilet. Eventually Mrs. Das relented when Mr. Das pointed out that he had given the girl her bath the night before. In the rearview mirror Mr. Kapasi watched as Mrs. Das emerged slowly from his bulky white Ambassador, dragging her shaved, largely bare legs across the back seat. She did not hold the little girl's hand as they walked to the rest room.

They were on their way to see the Sun Temple at Konarak. It was a dry, bright Saturday, the mid-July heat tempered by a steady ocean breeze, ideal weather for sightseeing. Ordinarily Mr. Kapasi would not have stopped so soon along the way, but less than five minutes after he'd picked up the family that morning in front of Hotel Sandy Villa, the little girl had complained. The first thing Mr. Kapasi had noticed when he saw Mr. and Mrs. Das, standing with their children under the portico of the hotel, was that they were very young, perhaps not even thirty. In addition to Tina they had two boys, Ronny and Bobby, who appeared very close in age and had teeth covered in a network of flashing silver wires. The family looked Indian but dressed as foreigners did, the children in stiff, brightly colored clothing and caps with translucent visors. Mr. Kapasi was accustomed to foreign tourists; he was assigned to them regularly because he could speak English. Yesterday he had driven an elderly couple from Scotland, both with spotted faces and fluffy white hair so thin it exposed their sunburnt scalps. In comparison, the tanned, youthful faces of Mr. and Mrs. Das were all the more striking. When he'd introduced himself, Mr. Kapasi had pressed his palms together in greeting, but Mr. Das squeezed hands like an American so that Mr. Kapasi felt it in his elbow. Mrs. Das, for her part, had flexed one side of her mouth, smiling dutifully at Mr. Kapasi, without displaying any interest in him.

As they waited at the tea stall, Ronny, who looked like the older of the two boys, clambered suddenly out of the back seat, intrigued by a goat tied to a stake in the ground.

"Don't touch it," Mr. Das said. He glanced up from his paperback tour book, which said "INDIA" in yellow letters and looked as if it had been published abroad. His voice, somehow tentative and a little shrill, sounded as though it had not yet settled into maturity.

"I want to give it a piece of gum," the boy called back as he trotted ahead.

Mr. Das stepped out of the car and stretched his legs by squatting briefly to the ground. A clean-shaven man, he looked exactly like a magnified version of Ronny. He had a sapphire blue visor, and was dressed in shorts, sneakers, and a T-shirt. The camera slung around his neck, with an impressive tele-photo lens and numerous buttons and markings, was the only complicated thing he wore. He frowned, watching as Ronny rushed toward the goat, but appeared to have no intention of intervening. "Bobby, make sure that your brother doesn't do anything stupid."

"I don't feel like it," Bobby said, not moving. He was sitting in the front seat beside Mr. Kapasi, studying a picture of the elephant god taped to the glove compartment.

"No need to worry," Mr. Kapasi said. "They are quite tame." Mr. Kapasi was forty-six years old, with receding hair that had gone completely silver, but his butterscotch complexion and his unlined brow, which he treated in spare moments to dabs of lotus-oil balm, made it easy to imagine what he must have looked like at an earlier age. He wore gray trousers and a matching jacket-style shirt, tapered at the waist, with short sleeves and a large pointed collar, made of a thin but durable synthetic material. He had specified both the cut and the fabric to his tailor — it was his preferred uniform for giving tours because it did not get crushed during his long hours behind the wheel. Through the windshield he watched as Ronny circled around the goat, touched it quickly on its side, then trotted back to the car.

"You left India as a child?" Mr. Kapasi asked when Mr. Das had settled once again into the passenger seat.

"Oh, Mina and I were both born in America," Mr. Das announced with an air of sudden confidence. "Born and raised. Our parents live here now, in Assansol. They retired. We visit them every couple years." He turned to watch as the little girl ran toward the car, the wide purple bows of her sundress flopping on her narrow brown shoulders. She was holding to her chest a doll with yellow hair that looked as if it had been chopped, as a punitive measure, with a pair of dull scissors. "This is Tina's first trip to India, isn't it, Tina?"

"I don't have to go to the bathroom anymore," Tina announced.

"Where's Mina?" Mr. Das asked.

Mr. Kapasi found it strange that Mr. Das should refer to his wife by her first name when speaking to the little girl. Tina pointed to where Mrs. Das was purchasing something from one of the shirtless men who worked at the tea stall. Mr. Kapasi heard one of the shirtless men sing a phrase from a popular Hindi love song as Mrs. Das walked back to the car, but she did not appear to understand the words of the song, for she did not express irritation, or embarrassment, or react in any other way to the man's declarations.

He observed her. She wore a red-and-white-checkered skirt that stopped above her knees, slip-on shoes with a square wooden heel, and a close-fitting blouse styled like a man's undershirt. The blouse was decorated at chest-level with a calico appliqué in the shape of a strawberry. She was a short woman, with small hands like paws, her frosty pink fingernails painted to match her lips, and was slightly plump in her figure. Her hair, shorn only a little longer than her husband's, was parted far to one side. She was wearing large dark brown sunglasses with a pinkish tint to them, and carried a big straw bag, almost as big as her torso, shaped like a bowl, with a water bottle poking out of it. She walked slowly, carrying some puffed rice tossed with peanuts and chili peppers in a large packet made from newspapers. Mr. Kapasi turned to Mr. Das.

"Where in America do you live?"

"New Brunswick, New Jersey."

"Next to New York?"

"Exactly. I teach middle school there."

"What subject?"

"Science. In fact, every year I take my students on a trip to the Museum of Natural History in New York City. In a way we have a lot in common, you could say, you and I. How long have you been a tour guide, Mr. Kapasi?"

"Five years."

Mrs. Das reached the car. "How long's the trip?" she asked, shutting the door.

"About two and a half hours," Mr. Kapasi replied.

At this Mrs. Das gave an impatient sigh, as if she had been traveling her whole life without pause. She fanned herself with a folded Bombay film magazine written in English.

"I thought that the Sun Temple is only eighteen miles north of Puri," Mr. Das said, tapping on the tour book.

"The roads to Konarak are poor. Actually it is a distance of fifty-two miles," Mr. Kapasi explained.

Mr. Das nodded, readjusting the camera strap where it had begun to chafe the back of his neck.

Before starting the ignition, Mr. Kapasi reached back to make sure the cranklike locks on the inside of each of the back doors were secured. As soon as the car began to move the little girl began to play with the lock on her side, clicking it with some effort forward and backward, but Mrs. Das said nothing to stop her. She sat a bit slouched at one end of the back seat, not offering her puffed rice to anyone. Ronny and Tina sat on either side of her, both snapping bright green gum.

"Look," Bobby said as the car began to gather speed. He pointed with his finger to the tall trees that lined the road. "Look."

"Monkeys!" Ronny shrieked. "Wow!"

They were seated in groups along the branches, with shining black faces, silver bodies, horizontal eyebrows, and crested heads. Their long gray tails dangled like a series of ropes among the leaves. A few scratched themselves with black leathery hands, or swung their feet, staring as the car passed.

"We call them the hanuman," Mr. Kapasi said. "They are quite common in the area."

As soon as he spoke, one of the monkeys leaped into the middle of the road, causing Mr. Kapasi to brake suddenly. Another bounced onto the hood of the car, then sprang away. Mr. Kapasi beeped his horn. The children began to get excited, sucking in their breath and covering their faces partly with their hands. They had never seen monkeys outside of a zoo, Mr. Das explained. He asked Mr. Kapasi to stop the car so that he could take a picture.

While Mr. Das adjusted his telephoto lens, Mrs. Das reached into her straw bag and pulled out a bottle of colorless nail polish, which she proceeded to stroke on the tip of her index finger.

The little girl stuck out a hand. "Mine too. Mommy, do mine too."

"Leave me alone," Mrs. Das said, blowing on her nail and turning her body slightly. "You're making me mess up."

The little girl occupied herself by buttoning and unbuttoning a pinafore on the doll's plastic body.

"All set," Mr. Das said, replacing the lens cap.

The car rattled considerably as it raced along the dusty road, causing them all to pop up from their seats every now and then, but Mrs. Das continued to polish her nails. Mr. Kapasi eased up on the accelerator, hoping to produce a smoother ride. When he reached for the gearshift the boy in front accommodated him by swinging his hairless knees out of the way. Mr. Kapasi noted that this boy was slightly paler than the other children. "Daddy, why is the driver sitting on the wrong side in this car, too?" the boy asked.

"They all do that here, dummy," Ronny said.

"Don't call your brother a dummy," Mr. Das said. He turned to Mr. Kapasi. "In America, you know . . . it confuses them."

"Oh yes, I am well aware," Mr. Kapasi said. As delicately as he could, he shifted gears again, accelerating as they approached a hill in the road. "I see it on *Dallas*, the steering wheels are on the left-hand side."

"What's *Dallas*?" Tina asked, banging her now naked doll on the seat behind Mr. Kapasi.

"It went off the air," Mr. Das explained. "It's a television show."

They were all like siblings, Mr. Kapasi thought as they passed a row of date trees. Mr. and Mrs. Das behaved like an older brother and sister, not parents. It seemed that they were in charge of the children only for the day; it was hard to believe they were regularly responsible for anything other than themselves. Mr. Das tapped on his lens cap, and his tour book, dragging his thumbnail occasionally across the pages so that they made a scraping sound. Mrs. Das continued to polish her nails. She had still not removed her sunglasses. Every now and then Tina renewed her plea that she wanted her nails done, too, and so at one point Mrs. Das flicked a drop of polish on the little girl's finger before depositing the bottle back inside her straw bag.

"Isn't this an air-conditioned car?" she asked, still blowing on her hand. The window on Tina's side was broken and could not be rolled down.

"Quit complaining," Mr. Das said. "It isn't so hot."

"I told you to get a car with air-conditioning," Mrs. Das continued. "Why do you do this, Raj, just to save a few stupid rupees. What are you saving us, fifty cents?"

Their accents sounded just like the ones Mr. Kapasi heard on American television programs, though not like the ones on *Dallas*.

"Doesn't it get tiresome, Mr. Kapasi, showing people the same thing every day?" Mr. Das asked, rolling down his own window all the way. "Hey, do you mind stopping the car. I just want to get a shot of this guy."

Mr. Kapasi pulled over to the side of the road as Mr. Das took a picture of a barefoot man, his head wrapped in a dirty turban, seated on top of a cart of grain sacks pulled by a pair of bullocks. Both the man and the bullocks were emaciated. In the back seat Mrs. Das gazed out another window, at the sky, where nearly transparent clouds passed quickly in front of one another.

"I look forward to it, actually," Mr. Kapasi said as they continued on their way. "The Sun Temple is one of my favorite places. In that way it is a reward for me. I give tours on Fridays and Saturdays only. I have another job during the week."

"Oh? Where?" Mr. Das asked.

"I work in a doctor's office."

"You're a doctor?"

"I am not a doctor. I work with one. As an interpreter."

"What does a doctor need an interpreter for?"

"He has a number of Gujarati patients. My father was Gujarati, but many people do not speak Gujarati in this area, including the doctor. And so the doctor asked me to work in his office, interpreting what the patients say."

"Interesting. I've never heard of anything like that," Mr. Das said.

Mr. Kapasi shrugged. "It is a job like any other."

"But so romantic," Mrs. Das said dreamily, breaking her extended silence. She lifted her pinkish brown sunglasses and arranged them on top of her head like a tiara. For the first time, her eyes met Mr. Kapasi's in the rearview mirror: pale, a bit small, their gaze fixed but drowsy.

Mr. Das craned to look at her. "What's so romantic about it?"

"I don't know. Something." She shrugged, knitting her brows together for an instant. "Would you like a piece of gum, Mr. Kapasi?" she asked brightly. She reached into her straw bag and handed him a small square wrapped in green-and-white-striped paper. As soon as Mr. Kapasi put the gum in his mouth a thick sweet liquid burst onto his tongue.

"Tell us more about your job, Mr. Kapasi," Mrs. Das said.

"What would you like to know, madame?"

"I don't know," she shrugged, munching on some puffed rice and licking the mustard oil from the corners of her mouth. "Tell us a typical situation." She settled back in her seat, her head tilted in a patch of sun, and closed her eyes. "I want to picture what happens."

"Very well. The other day a man came in with a pain in his throat."

"Did he smoke cigarettes?"

"No. It was very curious. He complained that he felt as if there were long pieces of straw stuck in his throat. When I told the doctor he was able to prescribe the proper medication."

"That's so neat."

"Yes," Mr. Kapasi agreed after some hesitation.

"So these patients are totally dependent on you," Mrs. Das said. She spoke slowly, as if she were thinking aloud. "In a way, more dependent on you than the doctor."

"How do you mean? How could it be?"

"Well, for example, you could tell the doctor that the pain felt like a burning, not straw. The patient would never know what you had told the doctor, and the doctor wouldn't know that you had told the wrong thing. It's a big responsibility."

"Yes, a big responsibility you have there, Mr. Kapasi," Mr. Das agreed.

Mr. Kapasi had never thought of his job in such complimentary terms. To him it was a thankless occupation. He found nothing noble in interpreting people's maladies, assiduously translating the symptoms of so many swollen bones, countless cramps of bellies and bowels, spots on people's palms that changed color, shape, or size. The doctor, nearly half his age, had an affinity for bell-bottom trousers and made humorless jokes about the Congress party. Together they worked in a stale little infirmary where Mr. Kapasi's smartly tailored clothes clung to him in the heat, in spite of the blackened blades of a ceiling fan churning over their heads.

The job was a sign of his failings. In his youth he'd been a devoted scholar of foreign languages, the owner of an impressive collection of dictionaries. He had dreamed of being an interpreter for diplomats and dignitaries, resolving conflicts between people and nations, settling disputes of which he alone could understand both sides. He was a self-educated man. In a series of notebooks, in the evenings before his parents settled his marriage, he had listed the common etymologies of words, and at one point in his life he was confident that he could converse, if given the opportunity, in English, French, Russian, Portuguese, and Italian, not to mention Hindi, Bengali, Orissi, and Gujarati. Now only a handful of European phrases remained in his memory, scattered words for things like saucers and chairs. English was the only non-Indian language he spoke fluently anymore. Mr. Kapasi knew it was not a remarkable talent. Sometimes he feared that his children knew better English than he did, just from watching television. Still, it came in handy for the tours.

He had taken the job as an interpreter after his first son, at the age of seven, contracted typhoid — that was how he had first made the acquaintance of the doctor. At the time Mr. Kapasi had been teaching English in a grammar school, and he bartered his skills as an interpreter to pay the increasingly exorbitant medical bills. In the end the boy had died one evening in his mother's arms, his limbs burning with fever, but then there was the funeral to pay for, and the other children who were born soon enough, and the newer, bigger house, and the good schools and tutors, and the fine shoes and the television, and the countless other ways he tried to console his wife and to keep her from crying in her sleep, and so when the doctor offered to pay him twice as much as he earned at the grammar school, he accepted. Mr. Kapasi knew that his wife had little regard for his career as an interpreter. He knew it reminded her of the son she'd lost, and that she resented the other lives he helped, in his own small way, to save. If ever she referred to his position, she used the phrase "doctor's assistant," as if the process of interpretation were equal to taking someone's temperature, or changing a bedpan. She never asked him about the patients who came to the doctor's office, or said that his job was a big responsibility.

For this reason it flattered Mr. Kapasi that Mrs. Das was so intrigued by his job. Unlike his wife, she had reminded him of its intellectual challenges. She had also used the word "romantic." She did not behave in a romantic way toward her husband, and yet she had used the word to describe him. He wondered if Mr. and Mrs. Das were a bad match, just as he and his wife were. Perhaps they, too, had little in common apart from three children and a decade of their lives. The signs he recognized from his own marriage were there — the bickering, the indifference, the protracted silences. Her sudden interest in him, an interest she did not express in either her husband or her children, was mildly intoxicating. When Mr. Kapasi thought once again about how she had said "romantic," the feeling of intoxication grew.

He began to check his reflection in the rearview mirror as he drove, feeling grateful that he had chosen the gray suit that morning and not the brown one, which tended to sag a little in the knees. From time to time he glanced through the mirror at Mrs. Das. In addition to glancing at her face he glanced at the strawberry between her breasts, and the golden brown hollow in her throat. He decided to tell Mrs. Das about another patient, and another: the young woman who had complained of a sensation of raindrops in her spine, the gentleman whose birthmark had begun to sprout hairs. Mrs. Das listened attentively, stroking her hair with a small plastic brush that resembled an oval bed of nails, asking more questions, for yet another example. The children were quiet, intent on spotting more monkeys in the trees, and Mr. Das was absorbed by his tour book, so it seemed like a private conversation between Mr. Kapasi and Mrs. Das. In this manner the next half hour passed, and when they stopped for lunch at a roadside restaurant that sold fritters and omelette sandwiches, usually something Mr. Kapasi looked forward to on his tours so that he could sit in peace and enjoy some hot tea, he was disappointed. As the Das family settled together under a magenta umbrella fringed with white and orange tassels, and placed their orders with one of the waiters who marched about in tricornered caps, Mr. Kapasi reluctantly headed toward a neighboring table.

"Mr. Kapasi, wait. There's room here," Mrs. Das called out. She gathered Tina onto her lap, insisting that he accompany them. And so, together, they had bottled mango juice and sandwiches and plates of onions and potatoes deep-fried in graham-flour batter. After finishing two omelette sandwiches Mr. Das took more pictures of the group as they ate.

"How much longer?" he asked Mr. Kapasi as he paused to load a new roll of film in the camera.

"About half an hour more."

By now the children had gotten up from the table to look at more monkeys perched in a nearby tree, so there was a considerable space between Mrs. Das and Mr. Kapasi. Mr. Das placed the camera to his face and squeezed one eye shut, his tongue exposed at one corner of his mouth. "This looks funny. Mina, you need to lean in closer to Mr. Kapasi."

She did. He could smell a scent on her skin, like a mixture of whiskey and rosewater. He worried suddenly that she could smell his perspiration, which he knew had collected beneath the synthetic material of his shirt. He polished off his mango juice in one gulp and smoothed his silver hair with his hands. A bit of the juice dripped onto his chin. He wondered if Mrs. Das had noticed.

She had not. "What's your address, Mr. Kapasi?" she inquired, fishing for something inside her straw bag.

"You would like my address?"

"So we can send you copies," she said. "Of the pictures." She handed him a scrap of paper which she had hastily ripped from a page of her film magazine. The blank portion was limited, for the narrow strip was crowded by lines of text and a tiny picture of a hero and heroine embracing under a eucalyptus tree.

The paper curled as Mr. Kapasi wrote his address in clear, careful letters. She would write to him, asking about his days interpreting at the doctor's office, and he would respond eloquently, choosing only the most entertaining anecdotes, ones that would make her laugh out loud as she read them in her house in New Jersey. In time she would reveal the disappointment of her marriage, and he his. In this way their friendship would grow, and flourish. He would possess a picture of the two of them, eating fried onions under a magenta umbrella, which he would keep, he decided, safely tucked between the pages of his Russian grammar. As his mind raced, Mr. Kapasi experienced a mild and pleasant shock. It was similar to a feeling he used to experience long ago when, after months of translating with the aid of a dictionary, he would finally read a passage from a French novel, or an Italian sonnet, and understand the words, one after another, unencumbered by his own efforts. In those moments Mr. Kapasi used to believe that all was right with the world, that all struggles were rewarded, that all of life's mistakes made sense in the end. The promise that he would hear from Mrs. Das now filled him with the same belief.

When he finished writing his address Mr. Kapasi handed her the paper, but as soon as he did so he worried that he had either misspelled his name, or accidentally reversed the numbers of his postal code. He dreaded the possibility of a lost letter, the photograph never reaching him, hovering somewhere in Orissa, close but ultimately unattainable. He thought of asking for the slip of paper again, just to make sure he had written his address accurately, but Mrs. Das had already dropped it into the jumble of her bag.

They reached Konarak at two-thirty. The temple, made of sandstone, was a massive pyramid-like structure in the shape of a chariot. It was dedicated to the great master of life, the sun, which struck three sides of the edifice as it made its journey each day across the sky. Twenty-four giant wheels were carved on the north and south sides of the plinth. The whole thing was drawn by a team of seven horses, speeding as if through the heavens. As they approached, Mr. Kapasi explained that the temple had been built between A.D. 1243 and 1255, with the efforts of twelve hundred artisans, by the great ruler of the Ganga dynasty, King Narasimhadeva the First, to commemorate his victory against the Muslim army.

"It says the temple occupies about a hundred and seventy acres of land," Mr. Das said, reading from his book.

"It's like a desert," Ronny said, his eyes wandering across the sand that stretched on all sides beyond the temple.

"The Chandrabhaga River once flowed one mile north of here. It is dry now," Mr. Kapasi said, turning off the engine.

They got out and walked toward the temple, posing first for pictures by the pair of lions that flanked the steps. Mr. Kapasi led them next to one of the wheels of the chariot, higher than any human being, nine feet in diameter.

"'The wheels are supposed to symbolize the wheel of life,'" Mr. Das read. "'They depict the cycle of creation, preservation, and achievement of realization.' Cool." He turned the page of his book. "'Each wheel is divided into eight thick and thin spokes, dividing the day into eight equal parts. The rims are carved with designs of birds and animals, whereas the medallions in the spokes are carved with women in luxurious poses, largely erotic in nature.'"

What he referred to were the countless friezes of entwined naked bodies, making love in various positions, women clinging to the necks of men, their knees wrapped eternally around their lovers' thighs. In addition to these were assorted scenes from daily life, of hunting and trading, of deer being killed with bows and arrows and marching warriors holding swords in their hands.

It was no longer possible to enter the temple, for it had filled with rubble years ago, but they admired the exterior, as did all the tourists Mr. Kapasi brought there, slowly strolling along each of its sides. Mr. Das trailed behind, taking pictures. The children ran ahead, pointing to figures of naked people, intrigued in particular by the Nagamithunas, the half-human, half-serpentine couples who were said, Mr. Kapasi told them, to live in the deepest waters of the sea. Mr. Kapasi was pleased that they liked the temple, pleased especially that it appealed to Mrs. Das. She stopped every three or four paces, staring silently at the carved lovers, and the processions of elephants, and the topless female musicians beating on two-sided drums.

Though Mr. Kapasi had been to the temple countless times, it occurred to him, as he, too, gazed at the topless women, that he had never seen his own wife fully naked. Even when they had made love she kept the panels of her blouse hooked together, the string of her petticoat knotted around her waist. He had never admired the backs of his wife's legs the way he now admired those of Mrs. Das, walking as if for his benefit alone. He had, of course, seen plenty of bare limbs before, belonging to the American and European ladies who took his tours. But Mrs. Das was different. Unlike the other women, who had an interest only in the temple, and kept their noses buried in a guidebook, or their eyes behind the lens of a camera, Mrs. Das had taken an interest in him.

Mr. Kapasi was anxious to be alone with her, to continue their private conversation, yet he felt nervous to walk at her side. She was lost behind her sunglasses, ignoring her husband's requests that she pose for another picture, walking past her children as if they were strangers. Worried that he might disturb her, Mr. Kapasi walked ahead, to admire, as he always did, the three life-sized bronze avatars of Surya, the sun god, each emerging from its own niche on the temple facade to greet the sun at dawn, noon, and evening. They wore elaborate headdresses, their languid, elongated eyes closed, their bare chests draped with carved chains and amulets. Hibiscus petals, offerings from previous visitors, were strewn at their gray-green feet. The last statue, on the northern wall of the temple, was Mr. Kapasi's favorite. This Surya had a tired expression, weary after a hard day of work, sitting astride a horse with folded legs. Even his horse's eyes were drowsy. Around his body were smaller sculptures of women in pairs, their hips thrust to one side.

"Who's that?" Mrs. Das asked. He was startled to see that she was standing beside him.

"He is the Astachala-Surya," Mr. Kapasi said. "The setting sun."

"So in a couple of hours the sun will set right here?" She slipped a foot out of one of her square-heeled shoes, rubbed her toes on the back of her other leg.

"That is correct."

She raised her sunglasses for a moment, then put them back on again. "Neat."

Mr. Kapasi was not certain exactly what the word suggested, but he had a feeling it was a favorable response. He hoped that Mrs. Das had understood Surya's beauty, his power. Perhaps they would discuss it further in their letters. He would explain things to her, things about India, and she would explain things to him about America. In its own way this correspondence would fulfill his dream, of serving as an interpreter between nations. He looked at her straw bag, delighted that his address lay nestled among its contents. When he pictured her so many thousands of miles away he plummeted, so much so that he had an overwhelming urge to wrap his arms around her, to freeze with her, even for an instant, in an embrace witnessed by his favorite Surya. But Mrs. Das had already started walking.

"When do you return to America?" he asked, trying to sound placid.

"In ten days."

He calculated: A week to settle in, a week to develop the pictures, a few days to compose her letter, two weeks to get to India by air. According to his schedule, allowing room for delays, he would hear from Mrs. Das in approximately six weeks' time.

The family was silent as Mr. Kapasi drove them back, a little past four-thirty, to Hotel Sandy Villa. The children had bought miniature granite versions of the chariot's wheels at a souvenir stand, and they turned them round in their hands. Mr. Das continued to read his book. Mrs. Das untangled Tina's hair with her brush and divided it into two little ponytails.

Mr. Kapasi was beginning to dread the thought of dropping them off. He was not prepared to begin his six-week wait to hear from Mrs. Das. As he stole glances at her in the rear-view mirror, wrapping elastic bands around Tina's hair, he wondered how he might make the tour last a little longer. Ordinarily he sped back to Puri using a shortcut, eager to return home, scrub his feet and hands with sandalwood soap, and enjoy the evening newspaper and a cup of tea that his wife would serve him in silence. The thought of that silence, something to which he'd long been resigned, now oppressed him. It was then that he suggested visiting the hills at Udayagiri and Khandagiri, where a number of monastic dwellings were hewn out of the ground, facing one another across a defile. It was some miles away, but well worth seeing, Mr. Kapasi told them.

"Oh yeah, there's something mentioned about it in this book," Mr. Das said. "Built by a Jain king or something."

"Shall we go then?" Mr. Kapasi asked. He paused at a turn in the road. "It's to the left."

Mr. Das turned to look at Mrs. Das. Both of them shrugged.

"Left, left," the children chanted.

Mr. Kapasi turned the wheel, almost delirious with relief. He did not know what he would do or say to Mrs. Das once they arrived at the hills. Perhaps he would tell her what a pleasing smile she had. Perhaps he would compliment her strawberry shirt, which he found irresistibly becoming. Perhaps, when Mr. Das was busy taking a picture, he would take her hand.

He did not have to worry. When they got to the hills, divided by a steep path thick with trees, Mrs. Das refused to get out of the car. All along the path, dozens of monkeys were seated on stones, as well as on the branches of the trees. Their hind legs were stretched out in front and raised to shoulder level, their arms resting on their knees.

"My legs are tired," she said, sinking low in her seat. "I'll stay here."

"Why did you have to wear those stupid shoes?" Mr. Das said. "You won't be in the pictures."

"Pretend I'm there."

"But we could use one of these pictures for our Christmas card this year. We didn't get one of all five of us at the Sun Temple. Mr. Kapasi could take it."

"I'm not coming. Anyway, those monkeys give me the creeps."

"But they're harmless," Mr. Das said. He turned to Mr. Kapasi. "Aren't they?"

"They are more hungry than dangerous," Mr. Kapasi said. "Do not provoke them with food, and they will not bother you."

Mr. Das headed up the defile with the children, the boys at his side, the little girl on his shoulders. Mr. Kapasi watched as they crossed paths with a Japanese man and woman, the only other tourists there, who paused for a final photograph, then stepped into a nearby car and drove away. As the car disappeared out of view some of the monkeys called out, emitting soft whooping sounds, and then walked on their flat black hands and feet up the path. At one point a group of them formed a little ring around Mr. Das and the children. Tina screamed in delight. Ronny ran in circles around his father. Bobby bent down and picked up a fat stick on the ground.

When he extended it, one of the monkeys approached him and snatched it, then briefly beat the ground.

"I'll join them," Mr. Kapasi said, unlocking the door on his side. "There is much to explain about the caves."

"No. Stay a minute," Mrs. Das said. She got out of the back seat and slipped in beside Mr. Kapasi. "Raj has his dumb book anyway." Together, through the windshield, Mrs. Das and Mr. Kapasi watched as Bobby and the monkey passed the stick back and forth between them.

"A brave little boy," Mr. Kapasi commented.

"It's not so surprising," Mrs. Das said.

"No?"

"He's not his."

"I beg your pardon?"

"Raj's. He's not Raj's son."

Mr. Kapasi felt a prickle on his skin. He reached into his shirt pocket for the small tin of lotus-oil balm he carried with him at all times, and applied it to three spots on his forehead. He knew that Mrs. Das was watching him, but he did not turn to face her. Instead he watched as the figures of Mr. Das and the children grew smaller, climbing up the steep path, pausing every now and then for a picture, surrounded by a growing number of monkeys.

"Are you surprised?" The way she put it made him choose his words with care.

"It's not the type of thing one assumes," Mr. Kapasi replied slowly. He put the tin of lotus-oil balm back in his pocket.

"No, of course not. And no one knows, of course. No one at all. I've kept it a secret for eight whole years." She looked at Mr. Kapasi, tilting her chin as if to gain a fresh perspective. "But now I've told you."

Mr. Kapasi nodded. He felt suddenly parched, and his forehead was warm and slightly numb from the balm. He considered asking Mrs. Das for a sip of water, then decided against it.

"We met when we were very young," she said. She reached into her straw bag in search of something, then pulled out a packet of puffed rice. "Want some?"

"No, thank you."

She put a fistful in her mouth, sank into the seat a little, and looked away from Mr. Kapasi, out the window on her side of the car. "We married when we were still in college. We were in high school when he proposed. We went to the same college, of course. Back then we couldn't stand the thought of being separated, not for a day, not for a minute. Our parents were best friends who lived in the same town. My entire life I saw him every weekend, either at our house or theirs. We were sent upstairs to play together while our parents joked about our marriage. Imagine! They never caught us at anything, though in a way I think it was all more or less a setup. The things we did those Friday and Saturday nights, while our parents sat downstairs drinking tea . . . I could tell you stories, Mr. Kapasi."

As a result of spending all her time in college with Raj, she continued, she did not make many close friends. There was no one to confide in about him at the end of a difficult day, or to share a passing thought or a worry. Her parents now lived on the other side of the world, but she had never been very close to them, anyway. After marrying so young she was overwhelmed by it all, having a child so quickly, and nursing, and warming up bottles of milk and testing their temperature against her wrist while Raj was at work, dressed in sweaters and corduroy pants, teaching his students about rocks and dinosaurs. Raj never looked cross or harried, or plump as she had become after the first baby.

Always tired, she declined invitations from her one or two

college girlfriends, to have lunch or shop in Manhattan. Eventually the friends stopped calling her, so that she was left at home all day with the baby, surrounded by toys that made her trip when she walked or wince when she sat, always cross and tired. Only occasionally did they go out after Ronny was born, and even more rarely did they entertain. Raj didn't mind; he looked forward to coming home from teaching and watching television and bouncing Ronny on his knee. She had been outraged when Raj told her that a Punjabi friend, someone whom she had once met but did not remember, would be staying with them for a week for some job interviews in the New Brunswick area.

Bobby was conceived in the afternoon, on a sofa littered with rubber teething toys, after the friend learned that a London pharmaceutical company had hired him, while Ronny cried to be freed from his playpen. She made no protest when the friend touched the small of her back as she was about to make a pot of coffee, then pulled her against his crisp navy suit. He made love to her swiftly, in silence, with an expertise she had never known, without the meaningful expressions and smiles Raj always insisted on afterward. The next day Raj drove the friend to JFK. He was married now, to a Punjabi girl, and they lived in London still, and every year they exchanged Christmas cards with Raj and Mina, each couple tucking photos of their families into the envelopes. He did not know that he was Bobby's father. He never would.

"I beg your pardon, Mrs. Das, but why have you told me this information?" Mr. Kapasi asked when she had finally finished speaking, and had turned to face him once again.

"For God's sake, stop calling me Mrs. Das. I'm twenty-eight. You probably have children my age."

"Not quite." It disturbed Mr. Kapasi to learn that she

thought of him as a parent. The feeling he had had toward her, that had made him check his reflection in the rearview mirror as they drove, evaporated a little.

"I told you because of your talents." She put the packet of puffed rice back into her bag without folding over the top.

"I don't understand," Mr. Kapasi said.

"Don't you see? For eight years I haven't been able to express this to anybody, not to friends, certainly not to Raj. He doesn't even suspect it. He thinks I'm still in love with him. Well, don't you have anything to say?"

"About what?"

"About what I've just told you. About my secret, and about how terrible it makes me feel. I feel terrible looking at my children, and at Raj, always terrible. I have terrible urges, Mr. Kapasi, to throw things away. One day I had the urge to throw everything I own out the window, the television, the children, everything. Don't you think it's unhealthy?"

He was silent.

"Mr. Kapasi, don't you have anything to say? I thought that was your job."

"My job is to give tours, Mrs. Das."

"Not that. Your other job. As an interpreter."

"But we do not face a language barrier. What need is there for an interpreter?"

"That's not what I mean. I would never have told you otherwise. Don't you realize what it means for me to tell you?"

"What does it mean?"

"It means that I'm tired of feeling so terrible all the time. Eight years, Mr. Kapasi, I've been in pain eight years. I was hoping you could help me feel better, say the right thing. Suggest some kind of remedy."

He looked at her, in her red plaid skirt and strawberry

T-shirt, a woman not yet thirty, who loved neither her husband nor her children, who had already fallen out of love with life. Her confession depressed him, depressed him all the more when he thought of Mr. Das at the top of the path, Tina clinging to his shoulders, taking pictures of ancient monastic cells cut into the hills to show his students in America, unsuspecting and unaware that one of his sons was not his own. Mr. Kapasi felt insulted that Mrs. Das should ask him to interpret her common, trivial little secret. She did not resemble the patients in the doctor's office, those who came glassy-eyed and desperate, unable to sleep or breathe or urinate with ease, unable, above all, to give words to their pains. Still, Mr. Kapasi believed it was his duty to assist Mrs. Das. Perhaps he ought to tell her to confess the truth to Mr. Das. He would explain that honesty was the best policy. Honesty, surely, would help her feel better, as she'd put it. Perhaps he would offer to preside over the discussion, as a mediator. He decided to begin with the most obvious question, to get to the heart of the matter, and so he asked, "Is it really pain you feel, Mrs. Das, or is it guilt?"

She turned to him and glared, mustard oil thick on her frosty pink lips. She opened her mouth to say something, but as she glared at Mr. Kapasi some certain knowledge seemed to pass before her eyes, and she stopped. It crushed him; he knew at that moment that he was not even important enough to be properly insulted. She opened the car door and began walking up the path, wobbling a little on her square wooden heels, reaching into her straw bag to eat handfuls of puffed rice. It fell through her fingers, leaving a zigzagging trail, causing a monkey to leap down from a tree and devour the little white grains. In search of more, the monkey began to follow Mrs. Das. Others joined him, so that she was soon being followed by about half a dozen of them, their velvety tails dragging behind.

Mr. Kapasi stepped out of the car. He wanted to holler, to alert her in some way, but he worried that if she knew they were behind her, she would grow nervous. Perhaps she would lose her balance. Perhaps they would pull at her bag or her hair. He began to jog up the path, taking a fallen branch in his hand to scare away the monkeys. Mrs. Das continued walking, oblivious, trailing grains of puffed rice. Near the top of the incline, before a group of cells fronted by a row of squat stone pillars, Mr. Das was kneeling on the ground, focusing the lens of his camera. The children stood under the arcade, now hiding, now emerging from view.

"Wait for me," Mrs. Das called out. "I'm coming."

Tina jumped up and down. "Here comes Mommy!"

"Great," Mr. Das said without looking up. "Just in time. We'll get Mr. Kapasi to take a picture of the five of us."

Mr. Kapasi quickened his pace, waving his branch so that the monkeys scampered away, distracted, in another direction.

"Where's Bobby?" Mrs. Das asked when she stopped.

Mr. Das looked up from the camera. "I don't know. Ronny, where's Bobby?"

Ronny shrugged. "I thought he was right here."

"Where is he?" Mrs. Das repeated sharply. "What's wrong with all of you?"

They began calling his name, wandering up and down the path a bit. Because they were calling, they did not initially hear the boy's screams. When they found him, a little farther down the path under a tree, he was surrounded by a group of monkeys, over a dozen of them, pulling at his T-shirt with their long black fingers. The puffed rice Mrs. Das had spilled was scattered at his feet, raked over by the monkeys' hands. The boy was silent, his body frozen, swift tears running down his startled face. His bare legs were dusty and red with welts from where one of the monkeys struck him repeatedly with the stick he had given to it earlier.

"Daddy, the monkey's hurting Bobby," Tina said.

Mr. Das wiped his palms on the front of his shorts. In his nervousness he accidentally pressed the shutter on his camera; the whirring noise of the advancing film excited the monkeys, and the one with the stick began to beat Bobby more intently. "What are we supposed to do? What if they start attacking?"

"Mr. Kapasi," Mrs. Das shrieked, noticing him standing to one side. "Do something, for God's sake, do something!"

Mr. Kapasi took his branch and shooed them away, hissing at the ones that remained, stomping his feet to scare them. The animals retreated slowly, with a measured gait, obedient but unintimidated. Mr. Kapasi gathered Bobby in his arms and brought him back to where his parents and siblings were standing. As he carried him he was tempted to whisper a secret into the boy's ear. But Bobby was stunned, and shivering with fright, his legs bleeding slightly where the stick had broken the skin. When Mr. Kapasi delivered him to his parents, Mr. Das brushed some dirt off the boy's T-shirt and put the visor on him the right way. Mrs. Das reached into her straw bag to find a bandage which she taped over the cut on his knee. Ronny offered his brother a fresh piece of gum. "He's fine. Just a little scared, right, Bobby?" Mr. Das said, patting the top of his head.

"God, let's get out of here," Mrs. Das said. She folded her arms across the strawberry on her chest. "This place gives me the creeps."

"Yeah. Back to the hotel, definitely," Mr. Das agreed.

"Poor Bobby, " Mrs. Das said. "Come here a second. Let Mommy fix your hair." Again she reached into her straw bag, this time for her hairbrush, and began to run it around the edges of the translucent visor. When she whipped out the hairbrush, the slip of paper with Mr. Kapasi's address on it fluttered away in the wind. No one but Mr. Kapasi noticed. He watched as it rose, carried higher and higher by the breeze, into the trees where the monkeys now sat, solemnly observing the scene below. Mr. Kapasi observed it too, knowing that this was the picture of the Das family he would preserve forever in his mind.

A Real Durwan

OORI MA, sweeper of the stairwell, had not slept in two nights. So the morning before the third night she shook the mites out of her bedding. She shook the quilts once underneath the letter boxes where she lived, then once again at the mouth of the alley, causing the crows who were feeding on vegetable peels to scatter in several directions.

As she started up the four flights to the roof, Boori Ma kept one hand placed over the knee that swelled at the start of every rainy season. That meant that her bucket, quilts, and the bundle of reeds which served as her broom all had to be braced under one arm. Lately Boori Ma had been thinking that the stairs were getting steeper; climbing them felt more like climbing a ladder than a staircase. She was sixty-four years old, with hair in a knot no larger than a walnut, and she looked almost as narrow from the front as she did from the side.

In fact, the only thing that appeared three-dimensional about Boori Ma was her voice: brittle with sorrows, as tart as curds, and shrill enough to grate meat from a coconut. It was with this voice that she enumerated, twice a day as she swept the stairwell, the details of her plight and losses suffered since her deportation to Calcutta after Partition. At that time, she maintained, the turmoil had separated her from a husband, four daughters, a two-story brick house, a rosewood *almari,* and a number of coffer boxes whose skeleton keys she still wore, along with her life savings, tied to the free end of her sari.

Aside from her hardships, the other thing Boori Ma liked to chronicle was easier times. And so, by the time she reached the second-floor landing, she had already drawn to the whole building's attention the menu of her third daughter's wedding night. "We married her to a school principal. The rice was cooked in rosewater. The mayor was invited. Everybody washed their fingers in pewter bowls." Here she paused, evened out her breath, and readjusted the supplies under her arm. She took the opportunity also to chase a cockroach out of the banister poles, then continued: "Mustard prawns were steamed in banana leaves. Not a delicacy was spared. Not that this was an extravagance for us. At our house, we ate goat twice a week. We had a pond on our property, full of fish."

By now Boori Ma could see some light from the roof spilling into the stairwell. And though it was only eight o'clock, the sun was already strong enough to warm the last of the cement steps under her feet. It was a very old building, the kind with bathwater that still had to be stored in drums, windows without glass, and privy scaffolds made of bricks.

"A man came to pick our dates and guavas. Another clipped hibiscus. Yes, there I tasted life. Here I eat my dinner from a rice pot." At this point in the recital Boori Ma's ears started to burn; a pain chewed through her swollen knee. "Have I mentioned that I crossed the border with just two bracelets on my wrist? Yet there was a day when my feet touched nothing but marble. Believe me, don't believe me, such comforts you cannot even dream them."

Whether there was any truth to Boori Ma's litanies no one

could be sure. For one thing, every day, the perimeters of her former estate seemed to double, as did the contents of her *almari* and coffer boxes. No one doubted she was a refugee; the accent in her Bengali made that clear. Still, the residents of this particular flat-building could not reconcile Boori Ma's claims to prior wealth alongside the more likely account of how she had crossed the East Bengal border, with the thousands of others, on the back of a truck, between sacks of hemp. And yet there were days when Boori Ma insisted that she had come to Calcutta on a bullock cart.

"Which was it, by truck or by cart?" the children sometimes asked her on their way to play cops and robbers in the alley. To which Boori Ma would reply, shaking the free end of her sari so that the skeleton keys rattled, "Why demand specifics? Why scrape lime from a betel leaf? Believe me, don't believe me. My life is composed of such griefs you cannot even dream them."

So she garbled facts. She contradicted herself. She embellished almost everything. But her rants were so persuasive, her fretting so vivid, that it was not so easy to dismiss her.

What kind of landowner ended up sweeping stairs? That was what Mr. Dalal of the third floor always wondered as he passed Boori Ma on his way to and from the office, where he filed receipts for a wholesale distributor of rubber tubes, pipes, and valve fittings in the plumbing district of College Street.

Bechareh, she probably constructs tales as a way of mourning the loss of her family, was the collective surmise of most of the wives.

And "Boori Ma's mouth is full of ashes, but she is the victim of changing times" was the refrain of old Mr. Chatterjee. He had neither strayed from his balcony nor opened a newspaper since Independence, but in spite of this fact, or maybe because of it, his opinions were always highly esteemed.

The theory eventually circulated that Boori Ma had once worked as hired help for a prosperous *zamindar* back east, and was therefore capable of exaggerating her past at such elaborate lengths and heights. Her throaty impostures hurt no one. All agreed that she was a superb entertainer. In exchange for her lodging below the letter boxes, Boori Ma kept their crooked stairwell spotlessly clean. Most of all, the residents liked that Boori Ma, who slept each night behind the collapsible gate, stood guard between them and the outside world.

No one in this particular flat-building owned much worth stealing. The second-floor widow, Mrs. Misra, was the only one with a telephone. Still, the residents were thankful that Boori Ma patrolled activities in the alley, screened the itinerant peddlers who came to sell combs and shawls from door to door, was able to summon a rickshaw at a moment's calling, and could, with a few slaps of her broom, rout any suspicious character who strayed into the area in order to spit, urinate, or cause some other trouble.

In short, over the years, Boori Ma's services came to resemble those of a real *durwan*. Though under normal circumstances this was no job for a woman, she honored the responsibility, and maintained a vigil no less punctilious than if she were the gatekeeper of a house on Lower Circular Road, or Jodhpur Park, or any other fancy neighborhood.

On the rooftop Boori Ma hung her quilts over the clothesline. The wire, strung diagonally from one corner of the parapet to the other, stretched across her view of television antennas, billboards, and the distant arches of Howrah Bridge. Boori Ma consulted the horizon on all four sides. Then she ran the tap at the base of the cistern. She washed her face, rinsed her feet, and rubbed two fingers over her teeth. After this she started to beat the quilts on each side with her broom. Every now and then she stopped and squinted at the cement, hoping to identify the culprit of her sleepless nights. She was so absorbed in this process that it was some moments before she noticed Mrs. Dalal of the third floor, who had come to set a tray of salted lemon peels out to dry in the sun.

"Whatever is inside this quilt is keeping me awake at night," Boori Ma said. "Tell me, where do you see them?"

Mrs. Dalal had a soft spot for Boori Ma; occasionally she gave the old woman some ginger paste with which to flavor her stews. "I don't see anything," Mrs. Dalal said after a while. She had diaphanous eyelids and very slender toes with rings on them.

"Then they must have wings," Boori Ma concluded. She put down her broom and observed one cloud passing behind another. "They fly away before I can squash them. But just see my back. I must be purple from their bites."

Mrs. Dalal lifted the drape of Boori Ma's sari, a cheap white weave with a border the color of a dirty pond. She examined the skin above and below her blouse, cut in a style no longer sold in shops. Then she said, "Boori Ma, you are imagining things."

"I tell you, these mites are eating me alive."

"It could be a case of prickly heat," Mrs. Dalal suggested.

At this Boori Ma shook the free end of her sari and made her skeleton keys rattle. She said, "I know prickly heat. This is not prickly heat. I haven't slept in three, perhaps four days. Who can count? I used to keep a clean bed. Our linens were muslin. Believe me, don't believe me, our mosquito nets were as soft as silk. Such comforts you cannot even dream them."

"I cannot dream them," Mrs. Dalal echoed. She lowered her diaphanous eyelids and sighed. "I cannot dream them, Boori Ma. I live in two broken rooms, married to a man who sells toilet parts." Mrs. Dalal turned away and looked at one of the quilts. She ran a finger over part of the stitching. Then she asked:

"Boori Ma, how long have you slept on this bedding?"

Boori Ma put a finger to her lips before replying that she could not remember.

"Then why no mention of it until today? Do you think it's beyond us to provide you with clean quilts? An oilcloth, for that matter?" She looked insulted.

"There is no need," Boori Ma said. "They are clean now. I beat them with my broom."

"I am hearing no arguments," Mrs. Dalal said. "You need a new bed. Quilts, a pillow. A blanket when winter comes." As she spoke Mrs. Dalal kept track of the necessary items by touching her thumb to the pads of her fingers.

"On festival days the poor came to our house to be fed," Boori Ma said. She was filling her bucket from the coal heap on the other side of the roof.

"I will have a word with Mr. Dalal when he returns from the office," Mrs. Dalal called back as she headed down the stairs. "Come in the afternoon. I will give you some pickles and some powder for your back."

"It's not prickly heat," Boori Ma said.

It was true that prickly heat was common during the rainy season. But Boori Ma preferred to think that what irritated her bed, what stole her sleep, what burned like peppers across her thinning scalp and skin, was of a less mundane origin.

She was ruminating on these things as she swept the stairwell — she always worked from top to bottom — when it started to rain. It came slapping across the roof like a boy in slippers too big for him and washed Mrs. Dalal's lemon peels into the gutter. Before pedestrians could open their umbrellas, it rushed down collars, pockets, and shoes. In that particular flat-building and all the neighboring buildings, creaky shutters were closed and tied with petticoat strings to the window bars.

At the time, Boori Ma was working all the way down on the second-floor landing. She looked up the ladderlike stairs, and as the sound of falling water tightened around her she knew her quilts were turning into yogurt.

But then she recalled her conversation with Mrs. Dalal. And so she continued, at the same pace, to sweep the dust, cigarette ends, and lozenge wrappers from the rest of the steps, until she reached the letter boxes at the bottom. To keep out the wind, she rummaged through her baskets for some newspapers and crammed them into the diamond-shaped openings of the collapsible gate. Then on her bucket of coals she set her lunch to boil, and monitored the flame with a plaited palm fan.

That afternoon, as was her habit, Boori Ma reknotted her hair, untied the loose end of her sari, and counted out her life savings. She had just woken from a nap of twenty minutes, which she had taken on a temporary bed made from newspapers. The rain had stopped and now the sour smell that rises from wet mango leaves was hanging low over the alley.

On certain afternoons Boori Ma visited her fellow residents. She enjoyed drifting in and out of the various households. The residents, for their part, assured Boori Ma that she was always welcome; they never drew the latch bars across their doors except at night. They went about their business, scolding children or adding up expenses or picking stones out of the evening rice. From time to time she was handed a glass of tea, the cracker tin was passed in her direction, and she helped children shoot chips across the carom board. Knowing not to sit on the furniture, she crouched, instead, in doorways and hallways, and observed gestures and manners in the same way a person tends to watch traffic in a foreign city.

On this particular afternoon Boori Ma decided to accept Mrs. Dalal's invitation. Her back still itched, even after napping on the newspapers, and she was beginning to want some prickly-heat powder after all. She picked up her broom — she never felt quite herself without it — and was about to climb upstairs, when a rickshaw pulled up to the collapsible gate.

It was Mr. Dalal. The years he had spent filing receipts had left him with purple crescents under his eyes. But today his gaze was bright. The tip of his tongue played between his teeth, and in the clamp of his thighs he held two small ceramic basins.

"Boori Ma, I have a job for you. Help me carry these basins upstairs." He pressed a folded handkerchief to his forehead and throat and gave the rickshaw driver a coin. Then he and Boori Ma carried the basins all the way up to the third floor. It wasn't until they were inside the flat that he finally announced, to Mrs. Dalal, to Boori Ma, and to a few other residents who had followed them out of curiosity, the following things: That his hours filing receipts for a distributor of rubber tubes, pipes, and valve fittings had ended. That the distributor himself, who craved fresher air, and whose profits had doubled, was opening a second branch in Burdwan. And that, following an assessment of his sedulous performance over the years, the distributor was promoting Mr. Dalal to manage the College Street branch. In his excitement on his way home through the plumbing district, Mr. Dalal had bought two basins.

"What are we supposed to do with two basins in a two-room flat?" Mrs. Dalal demanded. She had already been sulking over her lemon peels. "Who ever heard of it? I still cook on kerosene. You refuse to apply for a phone. And I have yet to see the fridge you promised when we married. You expect two basins to make up for all that?"

The argument that followed was loud enough to be heard

all the way down to the letter boxes. It was loud enough, and long enough, to rise above a second spell of rain that fell after dark. It was loud enough even to distract Boori Ma as she swept the stairwell from top to bottom for the second time that day, and for this reason she spoke neither of her hardships, nor of easier times. She spent the night on a bed of newspapers.

The argument between Mr. and Mrs. Dalal was still more or less in effect early the next morning, when a barefoot team of workmen came to install the basins. After a night of tossing and pacing, Mr. Dalal had decided to install one basin in the sitting room of their flat, and the other one on the stairwell of the building, on the first-floor landing. "This way everyone can use it," he explained from door to door. The residents were delighted; for years they had all brushed their teeth with stored water poured from mugs.

Mr. Dalal, meanwhile, was thinking: A sink on the stairwell is sure to impress visitors. Now that he was a company manager, who could say who might visit the building?

The workmen toiled for several hours. They ran up and down the stairs and ate their lunches squatting against the banister poles. They hammered, shouted, spat, and cursed. They wiped their sweat with the ends of their turbans. In general, they made it impossible for Boori Ma to sweep the stairwell that day.

To occupy the time, Boori Ma retired to the rooftop. She shuffled along the parapets, but her hips were sore from sleeping on newspapers. After consulting the horizon on all four sides, she tore what was left of her quilts into several strips and resolved to polish the banister poles at a later time.

By early evening the residents gathered to admire the day's labors. Even Boori Ma was urged to rinse her hands under the clear running water. She sniffed. "Our bathwater was scented with petals and attars. Believe me, don't believe me, it was a luxury you cannot dream."

Mr. Dalal proceeded to demonstrate the basin's various features. He turned each faucet completely on and completely off. Then he turned on both faucets at the same time, to illustrate the difference in water pressure. Lifting a small lever between the faucets allowed water to collect in the basin, if desired.

"The last word in elegance," Mr. Dalal concluded.

"A sure sign of changing times," Mr. Chatterjee reputedly admitted from his balcony.

Among the wives, however, resentment quickly brewed. Standing in line to brush their teeth in the mornings, each grew frustrated with having to wait her turn, for having to wipe the faucets after every use, and for not being able to leave her own soap and toothpaste tube on the basin's narrow periphery. The Dalals had their own sink; why did the rest of them have to share?

"Is it beyond us to buy sinks of our own?" one of them finally burst out one morning.

"Are the Dalals the only ones who can improve the conditions of this building?" asked another.

Rumors began spreading: that, following their argument, Mr. Dalal had consoled his wife by buying her two kilos of mustard oil, a Kashmiri shawl, a dozen cakes of sandalwood soap; that Mr. Dalal had filed an application for a telephone line; that Mrs. Dalal did nothing but wash her hands in her basin all day. As if this weren't enough, the next morning, a taxi bound for Howrah Station crammed its wheels into the alley; the Dalals were going to Simla for ten days.

"Boori Ma, I haven't forgotten. We will bring you back a sheep's-hair blanket made in the mountains," Mrs. Dalal said through the open window of the taxi. She was holding a leather purse in her lap which matched the turquoise border of her sari.

"We will bring two!" cried Mr. Dalal, who was sitting beside his wife, checking his pockets to make sure his wallet was in place.

Of all the people who lived in that particular flat-building, Boori Ma was the only one who stood by the collapsible gate and wished them a safe journey.

As soon as the Dalals were gone, the other wives began planning renovations of their own. One decided to barter a stack of her wedding bracelets and commissioned a white-washer to freshen the walls of the stairwell. Another pawned her sewing machine and summoned an exterminator. A third went to the silversmith and sold back a set of pudding bowls; she intended to have the shutters painted yellow.

Workers began to occupy this particular flat-building night and day. To avoid the traffic, Boori Ma took to sleeping on the rooftop. So many people passed in and out of the collapsible gate, so many others clogged the alley at all times, that there was no point in keeping track of them.

After a few days Boori Ma moved her baskets and her cook-ing bucket to the rooftop as well. There was no need to use the basin downstairs, for she could just as easily wash, as she always had, from the cistern tap. She still planned to polish the banister poles with the strips she had torn from her quilts. She continued to sleep on her newspapers.

More rains came. Below the dripping awning, a newspaper pressed over her head, Boori Ma squatted and watched the monsoon ants as they marched along the clothesline, carrying eggs in their mouths. Damper winds soothed her back. Her newspapers were running low.

Her mornings were long, her afternoons longer. She could not remember her last glass of tea. Thinking neither of her hardships nor of earlier times, she wondered when the Dalals would return with her new bedding.

She grew restless on the roof, and so for some exercise, Boori Ma started circling the neighborhood in the afternoons. Reed broom in hand, sari smeared with newsprint ink, she wandered through markets and began spending her life savings on small treats: today a packet of puffed rice, tomorrow some cashews, the day after that, a cup of sugarcane juice. One day she walked as far as the bookstalls on College Street. The next day she walked even farther, to the produce markets in Bow Bazaar. It was there, while she was standing in a shopping arcade surveying jackfruits and persimmons, that she felt something tugging on the free end of her sari. When she looked, the rest of her life savings and her skeleton keys were gone.

The residents were waiting for Boori Ma when she returned that afternoon at the collapsible gate. Baleful cries rang up and down the stairwell, all echoing the same news: the basin on the stairwell had been stolen. There was a big hole in the recently whitewashed wall, and a tangle of rubber tubes and pipes was sticking out of it. Chunks of plaster littered the landing. Boori Ma gripped her reed broom and said nothing.

In their haste the residents practically carried Boori Ma up the stairs to the roof, where they planted her on one side of the clothesline and started screaming at her from the other.

"This is all her doing," one of them hollered, pointing at Boori Ma. "She informed the robbers. Where was she when she was supposed to guard the gate?"

"For days she has been wandering the streets, speaking to strangers," another reported.

"We shared our coal, gave her a place to sleep. How could she betray us this way?" a third wanted to know.

Though none of them spoke directly to Boori Ma, she replied, "Believe me, believe me. I did not inform the robbers."

"For years we have put up with your lies," they retorted. "You expect us, now, to believe you?"

Their recriminations persisted. How would they explain it to the Dalals? Eventually they sought the advice of Mr. Chatterjee. They found him sitting on his balcony, watching a traffic jam.

One of the second-floor residents said, "Boori Ma has endangered the security of this building. We have valuables. The widow Mrs. Misra lives alone with her phone. What should we do?"

Mr. Chatterjee considered their arguments. As he thought things over, he adjusted the shawl that was wrapped around his shoulders and gazed at the bamboo scaffolding that now surrounded his balcony. The shutters behind him, colorless for as long as he could remember, had been painted yellow. Finally he said:

"Boori Ma's mouth is full of ashes. But that is nothing new. What is new is the face of this building. What a building like this needs is a real *durwan*."

So the residents tossed her bucket and rags, her baskets and reed broom, down the stairwell, past the letter boxes, through the collapsible gate, and into the alley. Then they tossed out Boori Ma. All were eager to begin their search for a real *durwan*.

From the pile of belongings Boori Ma kept only her broom. "Believe me, believe me," she said once more as her figure began to recede. She shook the free end of her sari, but nothing rattled.

Sexy

IT WAS A WIFE'S WORST NIGHTMARE. After nine years of marriage, Laxmi told Miranda, her cousin's husband had fallen in love with another woman. He sat next to her on a plane, on a flight from Delhi to Montreal, and instead of flying home to his wife and son, he got off with the woman at Heathrow. He called his wife, and told her he'd had a conversation that had changed his life, and that he needed time to figure things out. Laxmi's cousin had taken to her bed.

"Not that I blame her," Laxmi said. She reached for the Hot Mix she munched throughout the day, which looked to Miranda like dusty orange cereal. "Imagine. An English girl, half his age." Laxmi was only a few years older than Miranda, but she was already married, and kept a photo of herself and her husband, seated on a white stone bench in front of the Taj Mahal, tacked to the inside of her cubicle, which was next to Miranda's. Laxmi had been on the phone for at least an hour, trying to calm her cousin down. No one noticed; they worked for a public radio station, in the fund-raising department, and were surrounded by people who spent all day on the phone, soliciting pledges.

"I feel worst for the boy," Laxmi added. "He's been at home for days. My cousin said she can't even take him to school."

"It sounds awful," Miranda said. Normally Laxmi's phone conversations — mainly to her husband, about what to cook for dinner — distracted Miranda as she typed letters, asking members of the radio station to increase their annual pledge in exchange for a tote bag or an umbrella. She could hear Laxmi clearly, her sentences peppered every now and then with an Indian word, through the laminated wall between their desks. But that afternoon Miranda hadn't been listening. She'd been on the phone herself, with Dev, deciding where to meet later that evening.

"Then again, a few days at home won't hurt him." Laxmi ate some more Hot Mix, then put it away in a drawer. "He's something of a genius. He has a Punjabi mother and a Bengali father, and because he learns French and English at school he already speaks four languages. I think he skipped two grades."

Dev was Bengali, too. At first Miranda thought it was a religion. But then he pointed it out to her, a place in India called Bengal, in a map printed in an issue of *The Economist*. He had brought the magazine specially to her apartment, for she did not own an atlas, or any other books with maps in them. He'd pointed to the city where he'd been born, and another city where his father had been born. One of the cities had a box around it, intended to attract the reader's eye. When Miranda asked what the box indicated, Dev rolled up the magazine, and said, "Nothing you'll ever need to worry about," and he tapped her playfully on the head.

Before leaving her apartment he'd tossed the magazine in the garbage, along with the ends of the three cigarettes he always smoked in the course of his visits. But after she watched his car disappear down Commonwealth Avenue, back to his house in the suburbs, where he lived with his wife, Miranda retrieved it, and brushed the ashes off the cover, and rolled it in the opposite direction to get it to lie flat. She got into bed, still rumpled from their lovemaking, and studied the borders of Bengal. There was a bay below and mountains above. The map was connected to an article about something called the Gramin Bank. She turned the page, hoping for a photograph of the city where Dev was born, but all she found were graphs and grids. Still, she stared at them, thinking the whole while about Dev, about how only fifteen minutes ago he'd propped her feet on top of his shoulders, and pressed her knees to her chest, and told her that he couldn't get enough of her.

She'd met him a week ago, at Filene's. She was there on her lunch break, buying discounted pantyhose in the Basement. Afterward she took the escalator to the main part of the store, to the cosmetics department, where soaps and creams were displayed like jewels, and eye shadows and powders shimmered like butterflies pinned behind protective glass. Though Miranda had never bought anything other than a lipstick, she liked walking through the cramped, confined maze, which was familiar to her in a way the rest of Boston still was not. She liked negotiating her way past the women planted at every turn, who sprayed cards with perfume and waved them in the air; sometimes she would find a card days afterward, folded in her coat pocket, and the rich aroma, still faintly preserved, would warm her as she waited on cold mornings for the T.

That day, stopping to smell one of the more pleasing cards, Miranda noticed a man standing at one of the counters. He held a slip of paper covered in a precise, feminine hand. A saleswoman took one look at the paper and began to open drawers. She produced an oblong cake of soap in a black case, a hydrating mask, a vial of cell renewal drops, and two tubes of face cream. The man was tanned, with black hair that was visible on his knuckles. He wore a flamingo pink shirt, a navy blue suit, a camel overcoat with gleaming leather buttons. In order to pay he had taken off pigskin gloves. Crisp bills emerged from a burgundy wallet. He didn't wear a wedding ring.

"What can I get you, honey?" the saleswoman asked Miranda. She looked over the tops of her tortoiseshell glasses, assessing Miranda's complexion.

Miranda didn't know what she wanted. All she knew was that she didn't want the man to walk away. He seemed to be lingering, waiting, along with the saleswoman, for her to say something. She stared at some bottles, some short, others tall, arranged on an oval tray, like a family posing for a photograph.

"A cream," Miranda said eventually.

"How old are you?"

"Twenty-two."

The saleswoman nodded, opening a frosted bottle. "This may seem a bit heavier than what you're used to, but I'd start now. All your wrinkles are going to form by twenty-five. After that they just start showing."

While the saleswoman dabbed the cream on Miranda's face, the man stood and watched. While Miranda was told the proper way to apply it, in swift upward strokes beginning at the base of her throat, he spun the lipstick carousel. He pressed a pump that dispensed cellulite gel and massaged it into the back of his ungloved hand. He opened a jar, leaned over, and drew so close that a drop of cream flecked his nose.

Miranda smiled, but her mouth was obscured by a large brush that the saleswoman was sweeping over her face. "This is blusher Number Two," the woman said. "Gives you some color."

Miranda nodded, glancing at her reflection in one of the angled mirrors that lined the counter. She had silver eyes and skin as pale as paper, and the contrast with her hair, as dark and glossy as an espresso bean, caused people to describe her as striking, if not pretty. She had a narrow, egg-shaped head that rose to a prominent point. Her features, too, were narrow, with nostrils so slim that they appeared to have been pinched with a clothespin. Now her face glowed, rosy at the cheeks, smoky below the brow bone. Her lips glistened.

The man was glancing in a mirror, too, quickly wiping the cream from his nose. Miranda wondered where he was from. She thought he might be Spanish, or Lebanese. When he opened another jar, and said, to no one in particular, "This one smells like pineapple," she detected only the hint of an accent.

"Anything else for you today?" the saleswoman asked, accepting Miranda's credit card.

"No thanks."

The woman wrapped the cream in several layers of red tissue. "You'll be very happy with this product." Miranda's hand was unsteady as she signed the receipt. The man hadn't budged.

"I threw in a sample of our new eye gel," the saleswoman added, handing Miranda a small shopping bag. She looked at Miranda's credit card before sliding it across the counter. "Bye-bye, Miranda."

Miranda began walking. At first she sped up. Then, noticing the doors that led to Downtown Crossing, she slowed down.

"Part of your name is Indian," the man said, pacing his steps with hers.

She stopped, as did he, at a circular table piled with sweaters, flanked with pinecones and velvet bows. "Miranda?"

"Mira. I have an aunt named Mira."

His name was Dev. He worked in an investment bank back that way, he said, tilting his head in the direction of South Station. He was the first man with a mustache, Miranda decided, she found handsome.

They walked together toward Park Street station, past the kiosks that sold cheap belts and handbags. A fierce January wind spoiled the part in her hair. As she fished for a token in her coat pocket, her eyes fell to his shopping bag. "And those are for her?"

"Who?"

"Your Aunt Mira."

"They're for my wife." He uttered the words slowly, holding Miranda's gaze. "She's going to India for a few weeks." He rolled his eyes. "She's addicted to this stuff."

Somehow, without the wife there, it didn't seem so wrong. At first Miranda and Dev spent every night together, almost. He explained that he couldn't spend the whole night at her place, because his wife called every day at six in the morning, from India, where it was four in the afternoon. And so he left her apartment at two, three, often as late as four in the morning, driving back to his house in the suburbs. During the day he called her every hour, it seemed, from work, or from his cell phone. Once he learned Miranda's schedule he left her a message each evening at five-thirty, when she was on the T coming back to her apartment, just so, he said, she could hear his voice as soon as she walked through the door. "I'm thinking about you," he'd say on the tape. "I can't wait to see you." He told her he liked spending time in her apartment, with its kitchen counter no wider than a breadbox, and scratchy floors that sloped, and a buzzer in the lobby that always made a slightly embarrassing sound when he pressed it. He said he admired her for moving to Boston, where she knew no one, instead of remaining in Michigan, where she'd grown up and gone to college. When Miranda told him it was nothing to admire, that she'd moved to Boston precisely for that reason, he shook his head. "I know what it's like to be lonely," he said, suddenly serious, and at that moment Miranda felt that he understood her — understood how she felt some nights on the T, after seeing a movie on her own, or going to a bookstore to read magazines, or having drinks with Laxmi, who always had to meet her husband at Alewife station in an hour or two. In less serious moments Dev said he liked that her legs were longer than her torso, something he'd observed the first time she walked across a room naked. "You're the first," he told her, admiring her from the bed. "The first woman I've known with legs this long."

Dev was the first to tell her that. Unlike the boys she dated in college, who were simply taller, heavier versions of the ones she dated in high school, Dev was the first always to pay for things, and hold doors open, and reach across a table in a restaurant to kiss her hand. He was the first to bring her a bouquet of flowers so immense she'd had to split it up into all six of her drinking glasses, and the first to whisper her name again and again when they made love. Within days of meeting him, when she was at work, Miranda began to wish that there were a picture of her and Dev tacked to the inside of her cubicle, like the one of Laxmi and her husband in front of the Taj Mahal. She didn't tell Laxmi about Dev. She didn't tell anyone. Part of her wanted to tell Laxmi, if only because Laxmi was Indian, too. But Laxmi was always on the phone with her cousin these days, who was still in bed, whose husband was still in London, and whose son still wasn't going to school. "You must eat something," Laxmi would urge. "You mustn't lose your health." When she wasn't speaking to her cousin, she spoke to her husband, shorter conversations, in which she ended up arguing about whether to have chicken or lamb for dinner. "I'm sorry," Miranda heard her apologize at one point. "This whole thing just makes me a little paranoid."

Miranda and Dev didn't argue. They went to movies at the Nickelodeon and kissed the whole time. They ate pulled pork and cornbread in Davis Square, a paper napkin tucked like a cravat into the collar of Dev's shirt. They sipped sangria at the bar of a Spanish restaurant, a grinning pig's head presiding over their conversation. They went to the MFA and picked out a poster of water lilies for her bedroom. One Saturday, following an afternoon concert at Symphony Hall, he showed her his favorite place in the city, the Mapparium at the Christian Science center, where they stood inside a room made of glowing stained-glass panels, which was shaped like the inside of a globe, but looked like the outside of one. In the middle of the room was a transparent bridge, so that they felt as if they were standing in the center of the world. Dev pointed to India, which was red, and far more detailed than the map in *The Economist*. He explained that many of the countries, like Siam and Italian Somaliland, no longer existed in the same way; the names had changed by now. The ocean, as blue as a peacock's breast, appeared in two shades, depending on the depth of the water. He showed her the deepest spot on earth, seven miles deep, above the Mariana Islands. They peered over the bridge and saw the Antarctic archipelago at their feet, craned their necks and saw a giant metal star overhead. As Dev spoke, his voice bounced wildly off the glass, sometimes loud, sometimes soft, sometimes seeming to land in Miranda's chest, sometimes eluding her ear altogether. When a group of tourists walked onto the bridge, she could hear them clearing their throats, as if through microphones. Dev explained that it was because of the acoustics.

Miranda found London, where Laxmi's cousin's husband was, with the woman he'd met on the plane. She wondered which of the cities in India Dev's wife was in. The farthest Miranda had ever been was to the Bahamas once when she was a child. She searched but couldn't find it on the glass panels. When the tourists left and she and Dev were alone again, he told her to stand at one end of the bridge. Even though they were thirty feet apart, Dev said, they'd be able to hear each other whisper.

"I don't believe you," Miranda said. It was the first time she'd spoken since they'd entered. She felt as if speakers were embedded in her ears.

"Go ahead," he urged, walking backward to his end of the bridge. His voice dropped to a whisper. "Say something." She watched his lips forming the words; at the same time she heard them so clearly that she felt them under her skin, under her winter coat, so near and full of warmth that she felt herself go hot.

"Hi," she whispered, unsure of what else to say.

"You're sexy," he whispered back.

At work the following week, Laxmi told Miranda that it wasn't the first time her cousin's husband had had an affair. "She's decided to let him come to his senses," Laxmi said one evening as they were getting ready to leave the office. "She says it's for the boy. She's willing to forgive him for the boy." Miranda waited as Laxmi shut off her computer. "He'll come crawling back, and she'll let him," Laxmi said, shaking her head. "Not me. If my husband so much as looked at another woman I'd change the locks." She studied the picture tacked to her cubicle. Laxmi's husband had his arm draped over her shoulder, his knees leaning in toward her on the bench. She turned to Miranda. "Wouldn't you?"

She nodded. Dev's wife was coming back from India the next day. That afternoon he'd called Miranda at work, to say he had to go to the airport to pick her up. He promised he'd call as soon as he could.

"What's the Taj Mahal like?" she asked Laxmi.

"The most romantic spot on earth." Laxmi's face brightened at the memory. "An everlasting monument to love."

While Dev was at the airport, Miranda went to Filene's Basement to buy herself things she thought a mistress should have. She found a pair of black high heels with buckles smaller than a baby's teeth. She found a satin slip with scalloped edges and a knee-length silk robe. Instead of the pantyhose she normally wore to work, she found sheer stockings with a seam. She searched through piles and wandered through racks, pressing back hanger after hanger, until she found a cocktail dress made of a slinky silvery material that matched her eyes, with little chains for straps. As she shopped she thought about Dev, and about what he'd told her in the Mapparium. It was the first time a man had called her sexy, and when she closed her eyes she could still feel his whisper drifting through her body, under her skin. In the fitting room, which was just one big room with mirrors on the walls, she found a spot next to an older woman with a shiny face and coarse frosted hair. The woman stood barefoot in her underwear, pulling the black net of a body stocking taut between her fingers.

"Always check for snags," the woman advised.

Miranda pulled out the satin slip with scalloped edges. She held it to her chest.

The woman nodded with approval. "Oh yes."

"And this?" She held up the silver cocktail dress.

"Absolutely," the woman said. "He'll want to rip it right off you."

Miranda pictured the two of them at a restaurant in the South End they'd been to, where Dev had ordered foie gras and a soup made with champagne and raspberries. She pictured herself in the cocktail dress, and Dev in one of his suits, kissing her hand across the table. Only the next time Dev came to visit her, on a Sunday afternoon several days since the last time they'd seen each other, he was in gym clothes. After his wife came back, that was his excuse: on Sundays he drove into Boston and went running along the Charles. The first Sunday she opened the door in the knee-length robe, but Dev didn't even notice it; he carried her over to the bed, wearing sweatpants and sneakers, and entered her without a word. Later, she slipped on the robe when she walked across the room to get him a saucer for his cigarette ashes, but he complained that she was depriving him of the sight of her long legs, and demanded that she remove it. So the next Sunday she didn't bother. She wore jeans. She kept the lingerie at the back of a drawer, behind her socks and everyday underwear. The silver cocktail dress hung in her closet, the tag dangling from the seam. Often, in the morning, the dress would be in a heap on the floor; the chain straps always slipped off the metal hanger.

Still, Miranda looked forward to Sundays. In the mornings she went to a deli and bought a baguette and little containers of things Dev liked to eat, like pickled herring, and potato salad, and tortes of pesto and mascarpone cheese. They ate in bed, picking up the herring with their fingers and ripping the baguette with their hands. Dev told her stories about his childhood, when he would come home from school and drink mango juice served to him on a tray, and then play cricket by a lake, dressed all in white. He told her about how, at eighteen, he'd been sent to a college in upstate New York during something called the Emergency, and about how it took him years to be able to follow American accents in movies, in spite of the fact that he'd had an English-medium education. As he talked he smoked three cigarettes, crushing them in a saucer by the side of her bed. Sometimes he asked her questions, like how many lovers she'd had (three) and how old she'd been the first time (nineteen). After lunch they made love, on sheets covered with crumbs, and then Dev took a nap for twelve minutes. Miranda had never known an adult who took naps, but Dev said it was something he'd grown up doing in India, where it was so hot that people didn't leave their homes until the sun went down. "Plus it allows us to sleep together," he murmured mischievously, curving his arm like a big bracelet around her body.

Only Miranda never slept. She watched the clock on her bedside table, or pressed her face against Dev's fingers, intertwined with hers, each with its half-dozen hairs at the knuckle. After six minutes she turned to face him, sighing and stretching, to test if he was really sleeping. He always was. His ribs were visible through his skin as he breathed, and yet he was beginning to develop a paunch. He complained about the hair on his shoulders, but Miranda thought him perfect, and refused to imagine him any other way.

At the end of twelve minutes Dev would open his eyes as if he'd been awake all along, smiling at her, full of a contentment she wished she felt herself. "The best twelve minutes of the week." He'd sigh, running a hand along the backs of her calves. Then he'd spring out of bed, pulling on his sweatpants and lacing up his sneakers. He would go to the bathroom and brush his teeth with his index finger, something he told her all Indians knew how to do, to get rid of the smoke in his mouth. When she kissed him good-bye she smelled herself sometimes in his hair. But she knew that his excuse, that he'd spent the afternoon jogging, allowed him to take a shower when he got home, first thing.

Apart from Laxmi and Dev, the only Indians whom Miranda had known were a family in the neighborhood where she'd grown up, named the Dixits. Much to the amusement of the neighborhood children, including Miranda, but not including the Dixit children, Mr. Dixit would jog each evening along the flat winding streets of their development in his everyday shirt and trousers, his only concession to athletic apparel a pair of cheap Keds. Every weekend, the family — mother, father, two boys, and a girl — piled into their car and went away, to where nobody knew. The fathers complained that Mr. Dixit did not fertilize his lawn properly, did not rake his leaves on time, and agreed that the Dixits' house, the only one with vinyl siding, detracted from the neighborhood's charm. The mothers never invited Mrs. Dixit to join them around the Armstrongs' swimming pool. Waiting for the school bus with the Dixit children standing to one side, the other children would say "The Dixits dig shit," under their breath, and then burst into laughter.

One year, all the neighborhood children were invited to the birthday party of the Dixit girl. Miranda remembered a heavy aroma of incense and onions in the house, and a pile of shoes heaped by the front door. But most of all she remembered a piece of fabric, about the size of a pillowcase, which hung from a wooden dowel at the bottom of the stairs. It was a painting of a naked woman with a red face shaped like a knight's shield. She had enormous white eyes that tilted toward her temples, and mere dots for pupils. Two circles, with the same dots at their centers, indicated her breasts. In one hand she brandished a dagger. With one foot she crushed a struggling man on the ground. Around her body was a necklace composed of bleeding heads, strung together like a popcorn chain. She stuck her tongue out at Miranda.

"It is the goddess Kali," Mrs. Dixit explained brightly, shifting the dowel slightly in order to straighten the image. Mrs. Dixit's hands were painted with henna, an intricate pattern of zigzags and stars. "Come please, time for cake."

Miranda, then nine years old, had been too frightened to eat the cake. For months afterward she'd been too frightened even to walk on the same side of the street as the Dixits' house, which she had to pass twice daily, once to get to the bus stop, and once again to come home. For a while she even held her breath until she reached the next lawn, just as she did when the school bus passed a cemetery.

It shamed her now. Now, when she and Dev made love, Miranda closed her eyes and saw deserts and elephants, and marble pavilions floating on lakes beneath a full moon. One Saturday, having nothing else to do, she walked all the way to Central Square, to an Indian restaurant, and ordered a plate of tandoori chicken. As she ate she tried to memorize phrases printed at the bottom of the menu, for things like "delicious" and "water" and "check, please." The phrases didn't stick in her mind, and so she began to stop from time to time in the foreign-language section of a bookstore in Kenmore Square, where she studied the Bengali alphabet in the Teach Yourself series. Once she went so far as to try to transcribe the Indian part of her name, "Mira," into her Filofax, her hand moving in unfamiliar directions, stopping and turning and picking up her pen when she least expected to. Following the arrows in the book, she drew a bar from left to right from which the letters hung; one looked more like a number than a letter, another looked like a triangle on its side. It had taken her several tries to get the letters of her name to resemble the sample letters in the book, and even then she wasn't sure if she'd written Mira or Mara. It was a scribble to her, but somewhere in the world, she realized with a shock, it meant something.

During the week it wasn't so bad. Work kept her busy, and she and Laxmi had begun having lunch together at a new Indian restaurant around the corner, during which Laxmi reported the latest status of her cousin's marriage. Sometimes Miranda tried to change the topic; it made her feel the way she once felt in college, when she and her boyfriend at the time had walked away from a crowded house of pancakes without paying for their food, just to see if they could get away with it. But Laxmi spoke of nothing else. "If I were her I'd fly straight to London and shoot them both," she announced one day. She snapped a papadum in half and dipped it into chutney. "I don't know how she can just wait this way."

Miranda knew how to wait. In the evenings she sat at her dining table and coated her nails with clear nail polish, and ate salad straight from the salad bowl, and watched television, and waited for Sunday. Saturdays were the worst because by Saturday it seemed that Sunday would never come. One Saturday when Dev called, late at night, she heard people laughing and talking in the background, so many that she asked him if he was at a concert hall. But he was only calling from his house in the suburbs. "I can't hear you that well," he said. "We have guests. Miss me?" She looked at the television screen, a sitcom that she'd muted with the remote control when the phone rang. She pictured him whispering into his cell phone, in a room upstairs, a hand on the doorknob, the hallway filled with guests. "Miranda, do you miss me?" he asked again. She told him that she did.

The next day, when Dev came to visit, Miranda asked him what his wife looked like. She was nervous to ask, waiting until he'd smoked the last of his cigarettes, crushing it with a firm twist into the saucer. She wondered if they'd quarrel. But Dev wasn't surprised by the question. He told her, spreading some smoked whitefish on a cracker, that his wife resembled an actress in Bombay named Madhuri Dixit.

For an instant Miranda's heart stopped. But no, the Dixit girl had been named something else, something that began with P. Still, she wondered if the actress and the Dixit girl were related. She'd been plain, wearing her hair in two braids all through high school.

A few days later Miranda went to an Indian grocery in Central Square which also rented videos. The door opened to a complicated tinkling of bells. It was dinnertime, and she was the only customer. A video was playing on a television hooked up in a corner of the store: a row of young women in harem pants were thrusting their hips in synchrony on a beach.

"Can I help you?" the man standing at the cash register asked. He was eating a samosa, dipping it into some dark brown sauce on a paper plate. Below the glass counter at his waist were trays of more plump samosas, and what looked like pale, diamond-shaped pieces of fudge covered with foil, and some bright orange pastries floating in syrup. "You like some video?"

Miranda opened up her Filofax, where she had written "Mottery Dixit." She looked up at the videos on the shelves behind the counter. She saw women wearing skirts that sat low on the hips and tops that tied like bandannas between their breasts. Some leaned back against a stone wall, or a tree. They were beautiful, the way the women dancing on the beach were beautiful, with kohl-rimmed eyes and long black hair. She knew then that Madhuri Dixit was beautiful, too.

"We have subtitled versions, miss," the man continued. He wiped his fingertips quickly on his shirt and pulled out three titles.

"No," Miranda said. "Thank you, no." She wandered through the store, studying shelves lined with unlabeled packets and tins. The freezer case was stuffed with bags of pita bread and vegetables she didn't recognize. The only thing she recognized was a rack lined with bags and bags of the Hot Mix that Laxmi was always eating. She thought about buying some for Laxmi, then hesitated, wondering how to explain what she'd been doing in an Indian grocery.

"Very spicy," the man said, shaking his head, his eyes traveling across Miranda's body. "Too spicy for you."

By February, Laxmi's cousin's husband still hadn't come to his senses. He had returned to Montreal, argued bitterly with his wife for two weeks, packed two suitcases, and flown back to London. He wanted a divorce.

Miranda sat in her cubicle and listened as Laxmi kept telling her cousin that there were better men in the world, just waiting to come out of the woodwork. The next day the cousin said she and her son were going to her parents' house in California, to try to recuperate. Laxmi convinced her to arrange a weekend layover in Boston. "A quick change of place will do you good," Laxmi insisted gently, "besides which, I haven't seen you in years."

Miranda stared at her own phone, wishing Dev would call. It had been four days since their last conversation. She heard Laxmi dialing directory assistance, asking for the number of a beauty salon. "Something soothing," Laxmi requested. She scheduled massages, facials, manicures, and pedicures. Then she reserved a table for lunch at the Four Seasons. In her determination to cheer up her cousin, Laxmi had forgotten about the boy. She rapped her knuckles on the laminated wall.

"Are you busy Saturday?"

The boy was thin. He wore a yellow knapsack strapped across his back, gray herringbone trousers, a red V-necked sweater, and black leather shoes. His hair was cut in a thick fringe over his eyes, which had dark circles under them. They were the first thing Miranda noticed. They made him look haggard, as if he smoked a great deal and slept very little, in spite of the fact that he was only seven years old. He clasped a large sketch pad with a spiral binding. His name was Rohin.

"Ask me a capital," he said, staring up at Miranda.

She stared back at him. It was eight-thirty on a Saturday morning. She took a sip of coffee. "A what?"

"It's a game he's been playing," Laxmi's cousin explained. She was thin like her son, with a long face and the same dark circles under her eyes. A rust-colored coat hung heavy on her shoulders. Her black hair, with a few strands of gray at the temples, was pulled back like a ballerina's. "You ask him a country and he tells you the capital."

"You should have heard him in the car," Laxmi said. "He's already memorized all of Europe."

"It's not a game," Rohin said. "I'm having a competition with a boy at school. We're competing to memorize all the capitals. I'm going to beat him."

Miranda nodded. "Okay. What's the capital of India?"

"That's no good." He marched away, his arms swinging like a toy soldier. Then he marched back to Laxmi's cousin and tugged at a pocket of her overcoat. "Ask me a hard one."

"Senegal," she said.

"Dakar!" Rohin exclaimed triumphantly, and began running in larger and larger circles. Eventually he ran into the kitchen. Miranda could hear him opening and closing the fridge.

"Rohin, don't touch without asking," Laxmi's cousin called out wearily. She managed a smile for Miranda. "Don't worry, he'll fall asleep in a few hours. And thanks for watching him."

"Back at three," Laxmi said, disappearing with her cousin down the hallway. "We're double-parked."

Miranda fastened the chain on the door. She went to the kitchen to find Rohin, but he was now in the living room, at the dining table, kneeling on one of the director's chairs. He unzipped his knapsack, pushed Miranda's basket of manicure supplies to one side of the table, and spread his crayons over the surface. Miranda stood over his shoulder. She watched as he gripped a blue crayon and drew the outline of an airplane.

"It's lovely," she said. When he didn't reply, she went to the kitchen to pour herself more coffee.

"Some for me, please," Rohin called out.

She returned to the living room. "Some what?"

"Some coffee. There's enough in the pot. I saw."

She walked over to the table and sat opposite him. At times

he nearly stood up to reach for a new crayon. He barely made a dent in the director's chair.

"You're too young for coffee."

Rohin leaned over the sketch pad, so that his tiny chest and shoulders almost touched it, his head tilted to one side. "The stewardess let me have coffee," he said. "She made it with milk and lots of sugar." He straightened, revealing a woman's face beside the plane, with long wavy hair and eyes like asterisks. "Her hair was more shiny," he decided, adding, "My father met a pretty woman on a plane, too." He looked at Miranda. His face darkened as he watched her sip. "Can't I have just a little coffee? Please?"

She wondered, in spite of his composed, brooding expression, if he were the type to throw a tantrum. She imagined his kicking her with his leather shoes, screaming for coffee, screaming and crying until his mother and Laxmi came back to fetch him. She went to the kitchen and prepared a cup for him as he'd requested. She selected a mug she didn't care for, in case he dropped it.

"Thank you," he said when she put it on the table. He took short sips, holding the mug securely with both hands.

Miranda sat with him while he drew, but when she attempted to put a coat of clear polish on her nails he protested. Instead he pulled out a paperback world almanac from his knapsack and asked her to quiz him. The countries were arranged by continent, six to a page, with the capitals in boldface, followed by a short entry on the population, government, and other statistics. Miranda turned to a page in the Africa section and went down the list.

"Mali," she asked him.

"Bamako," he replied instantly.

"Malawi."

"Lilongwe."

She remembered looking at Africa in the Mapparium. She remembered the fat part of it was green.

"Go on," Rohin said.

"Mauritania."

"Nouakchott."

"Mauritius."

He paused, squeezed his eyes shut, then opened them, defeated. "I can't remember."

"Port Louis," she told him.

"Port Louis." He began to say it again and again, like a chant under his breath.

When they reached the last of the countries in Africa, Rohin said he wanted to watch cartoons, telling Miranda to watch them with him. When the cartoons ended, he followed her to the kitchen, and stood by her side as she made more coffee. He didn't follow her when she went to the bathroom a few minutes later, but when she opened the door she was startled to find him standing outside.

"Do you need to go?"

He shook his head but walked into the bathroom anyway. He put the cover of the toilet down, climbed on top of it, and surveyed the narrow glass shelf over the sink which held Miranda's toothbrush and makeup.

"What's this for?" he asked, picking up the sample of eye gel she'd gotten the day she met Dev.

"Puffiness."

"What's puffiness?"

"Here," she explained, pointing.

"After you've been crying?"

"I guess so."

Rohin opened the tube and smelled it. He squeezed a drop

of it onto a finger, then rubbed it on his hand. "It stings." He inspected the back of his hand closely, as if expecting it to change color. "My mother has puffiness. She says it's a cold, but really she cries, sometimes for hours. Sometimes straight through dinner. Sometimes she cries so hard her eyes puff up like bullfrogs."

Miranda wondered if she ought to feed him. In the kitchen she discovered a bag of rice cakes and some lettuce. She offered to go out, to buy something from the deli, but Rohin said he wasn't very hungry, and accepted one of the rice cakes. "You eat one too," he said. They sat at the table, the rice cakes between them. He turned to a fresh page in his sketch pad. "You draw."

She selected a blue crayon. "What should I draw?"

He thought for a moment. "I know," he said. He asked her to draw things in the living room: the sofa, the director's chairs, the television, the telephone. "This way I can memorize it."

"Memorize what?"

"Our day together." He reached for another rice cake.

"Why do you want to memorize it?"

"Because we're never going to see each other, ever again."

The precision of the phrase startled her. She looked at him, feeling slightly depressed. Rohin didn't look depressed. He tapped the page. "Go on."

And so she drew the items as best as she could — the sofa, the director's chairs, the television, the telephone. He sidled up to her, so close that it was sometimes difficult to see what she was doing. He put his small brown hand over hers. "Now me."

She handed him the crayon.

He shook his head. "No, now draw me."

"I can't," she said. "It won't look like you."

The brooding look began to spread across Rohin's face again, just as it had when she'd refused him coffee. "Please?"

She drew his face, outlining his head and the thick fringe of hair. He sat perfectly still, with a formal, melancholy expression, his gaze fixed to one side. Miranda wished she could draw a good likeness. Her hand moved in conjunction with her eyes, in unknown ways, just as it had that day in the bookstore when she'd transcribed her name in Bengali letters. It looked nothing like him. She was in the middle of drawing his nose when he wriggled away from the table.

"I'm bored," he announced, heading toward her bedroom. She heard him opening the door, opening the drawers of her bureau and closing them.

When she joined him he was inside the closet. After a moment he emerged, his hair disheveled, holding the silver cocktail dress. "This was on the floor."

"It falls off the hanger."

Rohin looked at the dress and then at Miranda's body. "Put it on."

"Excuse me?"

"Put it on."

There was no reason to put it on. Apart from in the fitting room at Filene's she had never worn it, and as long as she was with Dev she knew she never would. She knew they would never go to restaurants, where he would reach across a table and kiss her hand. They would meet in her apartment, on Sundays, he in his sweatpants, she in her jeans. She took the dress from Rohin and shook it out, even though the slinky fabric never wrinkled. She reached into the closet for a free hanger.

"Please put it on," Rohin asked, suddenly standing behind

her. He pressed his face against her, clasping her waist with both his thin arms. "Please?"

"All right," she said, surprised by the strength of his grip.

He smiled, satisfied, and sat on the edge of her bed.

"You have to wait out there," she said, pointing to the door. "I'll come out when I'm ready."

"But my mother always takes her clothes off in front of me."

"She does?"

Rohin nodded. "She doesn't even pick them up afterward. She leaves them all on the floor by the bed, all tangled.

"One day she slept in my room," he continued. "She said it felt better than her bed, now that my father's gone.''

"I'm not your mother," Miranda said, lifting him by the armpits off her bed. When he refused to stand, she picked him up. He was heavier than she expected, and he clung to her, his legs wrapped firmly around her hips, his head resting against her chest. She set him down in the hallway and shut the door. As an extra precaution she fastened the latch. She changed into the dress, glancing into the full-length mirror nailed to the back of the door. Her ankle socks looked silly, and so she opened a drawer and found the stockings. She searched through the back of the closet and slipped on the high heels with the tiny buckles. The chain straps of the dress were as light as paper clips against her collarbone. It was a bit loose on her. She could not zip it herself.

Rohin began knocking. "May I come in now?"

She opened the door. Rohin was holding his almanac in his hands, muttering something under his breath. His eyes opened wide at the sight of her. "I need help with the zipper," she said. She sat on the edge of the bed.

Rohin fastened the zipper to the top, and then Miranda

stood up and twirled. Rohin put down the almanac. "You're sexy," he declared.

"What did you say?"

"You're sexy."

Miranda sat down again. Though she knew it meant nothing, her heart skipped a beat. Rohin probably referred to all women as sexy. He'd probably heard the word on television, or seen it on the cover of a magazine. She remembered the day in the Mapparium, standing across the bridge from Dev. At the time she thought she knew what his words meant. At the time they'd made sense.

Miranda folded her arms across her chest and looked Rohin in the eyes. "Tell me something."

He was silent.

"What does it mean?"

"What?"

"That word. 'Sexy.' What does it mean?"

He looked down, suddenly shy. "I can't tell you."

"Why not?"

"It's a secret." He pressed his lips together, so hard that a bit of them went white.

"Tell me the secret. I want to know."

Rohin sat on the bed beside Miranda and began to kick the edge of the mattress with the backs of his shoes. He giggled nervously, his thin body flinching as if it were being tickled.

"Tell me," Miranda demanded. She leaned over and gripped his ankles, holding his feet still.

Rohin looked at her, his eyes like slits. He struggled to kick the mattress again, but Miranda pressed against him. He fell back on the bed, his back straight as a board. He cupped his hands around his mouth, and then he whispered, "It means loving someone you don't know."

Miranda felt Rohin's words under her skin, the same way

she'd felt Dev's. But instead of going hot she felt numb. It reminded her of the way she'd felt at the Indian grocery, the moment she knew, without even looking at a picture, that Madhuri Dixit, whom Dev's wife resembled, was beautiful.

"That's what my father did," Rohin continued. "He sat next to someone he didn't know, someone sexy, and now he loves her instead of my mother."

He took off his shoes and placed them side by side on the floor. Then he peeled back the comforter and crawled into Miranda's bed with the almanac. A minute later the book dropped from his hands, and he closed his eyes. Miranda watched him sleep, the comforter rising and falling as he breathed. He didn't wake up after twelve minutes like Dev, or even twenty. He didn't open his eyes as she stepped out of the silver cocktail dress and back into her jeans, and put the high-heeled shoes in the back of the closet, and rolled up the stockings and put them back in her drawer.

When she had put everything away she sat on the bed. She leaned toward him, close enough to see some white powder from the rice cakes stuck to the corners of his mouth, and picked up the almanac. As she turned the pages she imagined the quarrels Rohin had overheard in his house in Montreal. "Is she pretty?" his mother would have asked his father, wearing the same bathrobe she'd worn for weeks, her own pretty face turning spiteful. "Is she sexy?" His father would deny it at first, try to change the subject. "Tell me," Rohin's mother would shriek, "tell me if she's sexy." In the end his father would admit that she was, and his mother would cry and cry, in a bed surrounded by a tangle of clothes, her eyes puffing up like bullfrogs. "How could you," she'd ask, sobbing, "how could you love a woman you don't even know?"

As Miranda imagined the scene she began to cry a little herself. In the Mapparium that day, all the countries had seemed close enough to touch, and Dev's voice had bounced wildly off the glass. From across the bridge, thirty feet away, his words had reached her ears, so near and full of warmth that they'd drifted for days under her skin. Miranda cried harder, unable to stop. But Rohin still slept. She guessed that he was used to it now, to the sound of a woman crying.

On Sunday, Dev called to tell Miranda he was on his way. "I'm almost ready. I'll be there at two."

She was watching a cooking show on television. A woman pointed to a row of apples, explaining which were best for baking. "You shouldn't come today."

"Why not?"

"I have a cold," she lied. It wasn't far from the truth; crying had left her congested. "I've been in bed all morning."

"You do sound stuffed up." There was a pause. "Do you need anything?"

"I'm all set."

"Drink lots of fluids."

"Dev?"

"Yes, Miranda?"

"Do you remember that day we went to the Mapparium?"

"Of course."

"Do you remember how we whispered to each other?"

"I remember," Dev whispered playfully.

"Do you remember what you said?"

There was a pause. "'Let's go back to your place.'" He laughed quietly. "Next Sunday, then?"

The day before, as she'd cried, Miranda had believed she would never forget anything — not even the way her name looked written in Bengali. She'd fallen asleep beside Rohin and when she woke up he was drawing an airplane on the copy of

The Economist she'd saved, hidden under the bed. "Who's Deva-jit Mitra?" he had asked, looking at the address label.

Miranda pictured Dev, in his sweatpants and sneakers, laughing into the phone. In a moment he'd join his wife downstairs, and tell her he wasn't going jogging. He'd pulled a muscle while stretching, he'd say, settling down to read the paper. In spite of herself, she longed for him. She would see him one more Sunday, she decided, perhaps two. Then she would tell him the things she had known all along: that it wasn't fair to her, or to his wife, that they both deserved better, that there was no point in it dragging on.

But the next Sunday it snowed, so much so that Dev couldn't tell his wife he was going running along the Charles. The Sunday after that, the snow had melted, but Miranda made plans to go to the movies with Laxmi, and when she told Dev this over the phone, he didn't ask her to cancel them. The third Sunday she got up early and went out for a walk. It was cold but sunny, and so she walked all the way down Commonwealth Avenue, past the restaurants where Dev had kissed her, and then she walked all the way to the Christian Science center. The Mapparium was closed, but she bought a cup of coffee nearby and sat on one of the benches in the plaza outside the church, gazing at its giant pillars and its massive dome, and at the clear-blue sky spread over the city.

Mrs. Sen's

ELIOT HAD BEEN GOING to Mrs. Sen's for nearly a month, ever since school started in September. The year before he was looked after by a university student named Abby, a slim, freckled girl who read books without pictures on their covers, and refused to prepare any food for Eliot containing meat. Before that an older woman, Mrs. Linden, greeted him when he came home each afternoon, sipping coffee from a thermos and working on crossword puzzles while Eliot played on his own. Abby received her degree and moved off to another university, while Mrs. Linden was, in the end, fired when Eliot's mother discovered that Mrs. Linden's thermos contained more whiskey than coffee. Mrs. Sen came to them in tidy ballpoint script, posted on an index card outside the supermarket: "Professor's wife, responsible and kind, I will care for your child in my home." On the telephone Eliot's mother told Mrs. Sen that the previous baby-sitters had come to their house. "Eliot is eleven. He can feed and entertain himself; I just want an adult in the house, in case of an emergency." But Mrs. Sen did not know how to drive.

* * *

"As you can see, our home is quite clean, quite safe for a child," Mrs. Sen had said at their first meeting. It was a university apartment located on the fringes of the campus. The lobby was tiled in unattractive squares of tan, with a row of mailboxes marked with masking tape or white labels. Inside, intersecting shadows left by a vacuum cleaner were frozen on the surface of a plush pear-colored carpet. Mismatched remnants of other carpets were positioned in front of the sofa and chairs, like individual welcome mats anticipating where a person's feet would contact the floor. White drum-shaped lampshades flanking the sofa were still wrapped in the manufacturer's plastic. The TV and the telephone were covered by pieces of yellow fabric with scalloped edges. There was tea in a tall gray pot, along with mugs, and butter biscuits on a tray. Mr. Sen, a short, stocky man with slightly protuberant eyes and glasses with black rectangular frames, had been there, too. He crossed his legs with some effort, and held his mug with both hands very close to his mouth, even when he wasn't drinking. Neither Mr. nor Mrs. Sen wore shoes; Eliot noticed several pairs lined on the shelves of a small bookcase by the front door. They wore flip-flops. "Mr. Sen teaches mathematics at the university," Mrs. Sen had said by way of introduction, as if they were only distantly acquainted.

She was about thirty. She had a small gap between her teeth and faded pockmarks on her chin, yet her eyes were beautiful, with thick, flaring brows and liquid flourishes that extended beyond the natural width of the lids. She wore a shimmering white sari patterned with orange paisleys, more suitable for an evening affair than for that quiet, faintly drizzling August afternoon. Her lips were coated in a complementary coral gloss, and a bit of the color had strayed beyond the borders.

Yet it was his mother, Eliot had thought, in her cuffed, beige shorts and her rope-soled shoes, who looked odd. Her cropped hair, a shade similar to her shorts, seemed too lank and sensible, and in that room where all things were so carefully covered, her shaved knees and thighs too exposed. She refused a biscuit each time Mrs. Sen extended the plate in her direction, and asked a long series of questions, the answers to which she recorded on a steno pad. Would there be other children in the apartment? Had Mrs. Sen cared for children before? How long had she lived in this country? Most of all she was concerned that Mrs. Sen did not know how to drive. Eliot's mother worked in an office fifty miles north, and his father, the last she had heard, lived two thousand miles west.

"I have been giving her lessons, actually," Mr. Sen said, setting his mug on the coffee table. It was the first time he had spoken. "By my estimate Mrs. Sen should have her driver's license by December."

"Is that so?" Eliot's mother noted the information on her pad.

"Yes, I am learning," Mrs. Sen said. "But I am a slow student. At home, you know, we have a driver."

"You mean a chauffeur?"

Mrs. Sen glanced at Mr. Sen, who nodded.

Eliot's mother nodded, too, looking around the room. "And that's all . . . in India?"

"Yes," Mrs. Sen replied. The mention of the word seemed to release something in her. She neatened the border of her sari where it rose diagonally across her chest. She, too, looked around the room, as if she noticed in the lampshades, in the teapot, in the shadows frozen on the carpet, something the rest of them could not. "Everything is there."

Eliot didn't mind going to Mrs. Sen's after school. By September the tiny beach house where he and his mother lived year-round was already cold; Eliot and his mother had to bring a portable heater along whenever they moved from one room to another, and to seal the windows with plastic sheets and a hair drier. The beach was barren and dull to play on alone; the only neighbors who stayed on past Labor Day, a young married couple, had no children, and Eliot no longer found it interesting to gather broken mussel shells in his bucket, or to stroke the seaweed, strewn like strips of emerald lasagna on the sand. Mrs. Sen's apartment was warm, sometimes too warm; the radiators continuously hissed like a pressure cooker. Eliot learned to remove his sneakers first thing in Mrs. Sen's doorway, and to place them on the bookcase next to a row of Mrs. Sen's slippers, each a different color, with soles as flat as cardboard and a ring of leather to hold her big toe.

He especially enjoyed watching Mrs. Sen as she chopped things, seated on newspapers on the living room floor. Instead of a knife she used a blade that curved like the prow of a Viking ship, sailing to battle in distant seas. The blade was hinged at one end to a narrow wooden base. The steel, more black than silver, lacked a uniform polish, and had a serrated crest, she told Eliot, for grating. Each afternoon Mrs. Sen lifted the blade and locked it into place, so that it met the base at an angle. Facing the sharp edge without ever touching it, she took whole vegetables between her hands and hacked them apart: cauliflower, cabbage, butternut squash. She split things in half, then quarters, speedily producing florets, cubes, slices, and shreds. She could peel a potato in seconds. At times she sat cross-legged, at times with legs splayed, surrounded by an array of colanders and shallow bowls of water in which she immersed her chopped ingredients.

While she worked she kept an eye on the television and an eye on Eliot, but she never seemed to keep an eye on the blade. Nevertheless she refused to let Eliot walk around when she was chopping. "Just sit, sit please, it will take just two more minutes," she said, pointing to the sofa, which was draped at all times with a green and black bedcover printed with rows of elephants bearing palanquins on their backs. The daily procedure took about an hour. In order to occupy Eliot she supplied him with the comics section of the newspaper, and crackers spread with peanut butter, and sometimes a Popsicle, or carrot sticks sculpted with her blade. She would have roped off the area if she could. Once, though, she broke her own rule; in need of additional supplies, and reluctant to rise from the catastrophic mess that barricaded her, she asked Eliot to fetch something from the kitchen. "If you don't mind, there is a plastic bowl, large enough to hold this spinach, in the cabinet next to the fridge. Careful, oh dear, be careful," she cautioned as he approached. "Just leave it, thank you, on the coffee table, I can reach."

She had brought the blade from India, where apparently there was at least one in every household. "Whenever there is a wedding in the family," she told Eliot one day, "or a large celebration of any kind, my mother sends out word in the evening for all the neighborhood women to bring blades just like this one, and then they sit in an enormous circle on the roof of our building, laughing and gossiping and slicing fifty kilos of vegetables through the night." Her profile hovered protectively over her work, a confetti of cucumber, eggplant, and onion skins heaped around her. "It is impossible to fall asleep those nights, listening to their chatter." She paused to look at a pine tree framed by the living room window. "Here, in this place where Mr. Sen has brought me, I cannot sometimes sleep in so much silence."

Another day she sat prying the pimpled yellow fat off chicken parts, then dividing them between thigh and leg. As the bones cracked apart over the blade her golden bangles jostled, her forearms glowed, and she exhaled audibly through her nose. At one point she paused, gripping the chicken with both hands, and stared out the window. Fat and sinew clung to her fingers.

"Eliot, if I began to scream right now at the top of my lungs, would someone come?"

"Mrs. Sen, what's wrong?"

"Nothing. I am only asking if someone would come."

Eliot shrugged. "Maybe."

"At home that is all you have to do. Not everybody has a telephone. But just raise your voice a bit, or express grief or joy of any kind, and one whole neighborhood and half of another has come to share the news, to help with arrangements."

By then Eliot understood that when Mrs. Sen said home, she meant India, not the apartment where she sat chopping vegetables. He thought of his own home, just five miles away, and the young married couple who waved from time to time as they jogged at sunset along the shore. On Labor Day they'd had a party. People were piled on the deck, eating, drinking, the sound of their laughter rising above the weary sigh of the waves. Eliot and his mother weren't invited. It was one of the rare days his mother had off, but they didn't go anywhere. She did the laundry, and balanced the checkbook, and, with Eliot's help, vacuumed the inside of the car. Eliot had suggested that they go through the car wash a few miles down the road as they did every now and then, so that they could sit inside, safe and dry, as soap and water and a circle of giant canvas ribbons slapped the windshield, but his mother said she was too tired, and sprayed the car with a hose. When, by evening, the crowd on the neighbors' deck began dancing, she looked up their number in the phone book and asked them to keep it down.

"They might call you," Eliot said eventually to Mrs. Sen. "But they might complain that you were making too much noise."

From where Eliot sat on the sofa he could detect her curious scent of mothballs and cumin, and he could see the perfectly centered part in her braided hair, which was shaded with crushed vermilion and therefore appeared to be blushing. At first Eliot had wondered if she had cut her scalp, or if something had bitten her there. But then one day he saw her standing before the bathroom mirror, solemnly applying, with the head of a thumbtack, a fresh stroke of scarlet powder, which she stored in a small jam jar. A few grains of the powder fell onto the bridge of her nose as she used the thumbtack to stamp a dot above her eyebrows. "I must wear the powder every day," she explained when Eliot asked her what it was for, "for the rest of the days that I am married."

"Like a wedding ring, you mean?"

"Exactly, Eliot, exactly like a wedding ring. Only with no fear of losing it in the dishwater."

By the time Eliot's mother arrived at twenty past six, Mrs. Sen always made sure all evidence of her chopping was disposed of. The blade was scrubbed, rinsed, dried, folded, and stowed away in a cupboard with the aid of a stepladder. With Eliot's help the newspapers were crushed with all the peels and seeds and skins inside them. Brimming bowls and colanders lined the countertop, spices and pastes were measured and blended, and eventually a collection of broths simmered over periwinkle flames on the stove. It was never a special occasion, nor was she ever expecting company. It was merely dinner for herself and Mr. Sen, as indicated by the two plates and two glasses she set, without napkins or silverware, on the square Formica table at one end of the living room.

As he pressed the newspapers deeper into the garbage pail,

Eliot felt that he and Mrs. Sen were disobeying some unspoken rule. Perhaps it was because of the urgency with which Mrs. Sen accomplished everything, pinching salt and sugar between her fingernails, running water through lentils, sponging all imaginable surfaces, shutting cupboard doors with a series of successive clicks. It gave him a little shock to see his mother all of a sudden, in the transparent stockings and shoulder-padded suits she wore to her job, peering into the corners of Mrs. Sen's apartment. She tended to hover on the far side of the door frame, calling to Eliot to put on his sneakers and gather his things, but Mrs. Sen would not allow it. Each evening she insisted that his mother sit on the sofa, where she was served something to eat: a glass of bright pink yogurt with rose syrup, breaded mincemeat with raisins, a bowl of semolina halvah.

"Really, Mrs. Sen. I take a late lunch. You shouldn't go to so much trouble."

"It is no trouble. Just like Eliot. No trouble at all."

His mother nibbled Mrs. Sen's concoctions with eyes cast upward, in search of an opinion. She kept her knees pressed together, the high heels she never removed pressed into the pear-colored carpet. "It's delicious," she would conclude, setting down the plate after a bite or two. Eliot knew she didn't like the tastes; she'd told him so once in the car. He also knew she didn't eat lunch at work, because the first thing she did when they were back at the beach house was pour herself a glass of wine and eat bread and cheese, sometimes so much of it that she wasn't hungry for the pizza they normally ordered for dinner. She sat at the table as he ate, drinking more wine and asking how his day was, but eventually she went to the deck to smoke a cigarette, leaving Eliot to wrap up the leftovers.

*　*　*

Each afternoon Mrs. Sen stood in a grove of pine trees by the main road where the school bus dropped off Eliot along with two or three other children who lived nearby. Eliot always sensed that Mrs. Sen had been waiting for some time, as if eager to greet a person she hadn't seen in years. The hair at her temples blew about in the breeze, the column of vermilion fresh in her part. She wore navy blue sunglasses a little too big for her face. Her sari, a different pattern each day, fluttered below the hem of a checkered all-weather coat. Acorns and caterpillars dotted the asphalt loop that framed the complex of about a dozen brick buildings, all identical, embedded in a communal expanse of log chips. As they walked back from the bus stop she produced a sandwich bag from her pocket, and offered Eliot the peeled wedges of an orange, or lightly salted peanuts, which she had already shelled.

They proceeded directly to the car, and for twenty minutes Mrs. Sen practiced driving. It was a toffee-colored sedan with vinyl seats. There was an AM radio with chrome buttons, and on the ledge over the back seat, a box of Kleenex and an ice scraper. Mrs. Sen told Eliot she didn't feel right leaving him alone in the apartment, but Eliot knew she wanted him sitting beside her because she was afraid. She dreaded the roar of the ignition, and placed her hands over her ears to block out the sound as she pressed her slippered feet to the gas, revving the engine.

"Mr. Sen says that once I receive my license, everything will improve. What do you think, Eliot? Will things improve?"

"You could go places," Eliot suggested. "You could go anywhere."

"Could I drive all the way to Calcutta? How long would that take, Eliot? Ten thousand miles, at fifty miles per hour?"

Eliot could not do the math in his head. He watched Mrs.

Sen adjust the driver's seat, the rearview mirror, the sunglasses on top of her head. She tuned the radio to a station that played symphonies. "Is it Beethoven?" she asked once, pronouncing the first part of the composer's name not "bay," but "bee," like the insect. She rolled down the window on her side, and asked Eliot to do the same. Eventually she pressed her foot to the brake pedal, manipulated the automatic gear shift as if it were an enormous, leaky pen, and backed inch by inch out of the parking space. She circled the apartment complex once, then once again.

"How am I doing, Eliot? Am I going to pass?"

She was continuously distracted. She stopped the car without warning to listen to something on the radio, or to stare at something, anything, in the road. If she passed a person, she waved. If she saw a bird twenty feet in front of her, she beeped the horn with her index finger and waited for it to fly away. In India, she said, the driver sat on the right side, not the left. Slowly they crept past the swing set, the laundry building, the dark green trash bins, the rows of parked cars. Each time they approached the grove of pine trees where the asphalt loop met the main road, she leaned forward, pinning all her weight against the brake as cars hurtled past. It was a narrow road painted with a solid yellow stripe, with one lane of traffic in either direction.

"Impossible, Eliot. How can I go there?"

"You need to wait until no one's coming."

"Why will not anybody slow down?"

"No one's coming now."

"But what about the car from the right, do you see? And look, a truck is behind it. Anyway, I am not allowed on the main road without Mr. Sen."

"You have to turn and speed up fast," Eliot said. That was the way his mother did it, as if without thinking. It seemed so simple when he sat beside his mother, gliding in the evenings back to the beach house. Then the road was just a road, the other cars merely part of the scenery. But when he sat with Mrs. Sen, under an autumn sun that glowed without warmth through the trees, he saw how that same stream of cars made her knuckles pale, her wrists tremble, and her English falter.

"Everyone, this people, too much in their world."

Two things, Eliot learned, made Mrs. Sen happy. One was the arrival of a letter from her family. It was her custom to check the mailbox after driving practice. She would unlock the box, but she would ask Eliot to reach inside, telling him what to look for, and then she would shut her eyes and shield them with her hands while he shuffled through the bills and magazines that came in Mr. Sen's name. At first Eliot found Mrs. Sen's anxiety incomprehensible; his mother had a p.o. box in town, and she collected mail so infrequently that once their electricity was cut off for three days. Weeks passed at Mrs. Sen's before he found a blue aerogram, grainy to the touch, crammed with stamps showing a bald man at a spinning wheel, and blackened by postmarks.

"Is this it, Mrs. Sen?"

For the first time she embraced him, clasping his face to her sari, surrounding him with her odor of mothballs and cumin. She seized the letter from his hands.

As soon as they were inside the apartment she kicked off her slippers this way and that, drew a wire pin from her hair, and slit the top and sides of the aerogram in three strokes. Her eyes darted back and forth as she read. As soon as she was finished, she cast aside the embroidery that covered the telephone, dialed, and asked, "Yes, is Mr. Sen there, please? It is Mrs. Sen and it is very important."

Subsequently she spoke in her own language, rapid and

riotous to Eliot's ears; it was clear that she was reading the contents of the letter, word by word. As she read her voice was louder and seemed to shift in key. Though she stood plainly before him, Eliot had the sensation that Mrs. Sen was no longer present in the room with the pear-colored carpet.

Afterward the apartment was suddenly too small to contain her. They crossed the main road and walked a short distance to the university quadrangle, where bells in a stone tower chimed on the hour. They wandered through the student union, and dragged a tray together along the cafeteria ledge, and ate french fries heaped in a cardboard boat among students chatting at circular tables. Eliot drank soda from a paper cup, Mrs. Sen steeped a tea bag with sugar and cream. After eating they explored the art building, looking at sculptures and silk screens in cool corridors thick with the fragrance of wet paint and clay. They walked past the mathematics building, where Mr. Sen taught his classes.

They ended up in the noisy, chlorine-scented wing of the athletic building where, through a wide window on the fourth floor, they watched swimmers crossing from end to end in glaring turquoise pools. Mrs. Sen took the aerogram from India out of her purse and studied the front and back. She unfolded it and reread to herself, sighing every now and then. When she had finished she gazed for some time at the swimmers.

"My sister has had a baby girl. By the time I see her, depending if Mr. Sen gets his tenure, she will be three years old. Her own aunt will be a stranger. If we sit side by side on a train she will not know my face." She put away the letter, then placed a hand on Eliot's head. "Do you miss your mother, Eliot, these afternoons with me?"

The thought had never occurred to him.

"You must miss her. When I think of you, only a boy, separated from your mother for so much of the day, I am ashamed."

"I see her at night."

"When I was your age I was without knowing that one day I would be so far. You are wiser than that, Eliot. You already taste the way things must be."

The other thing that made Mrs. Sen happy was fish from the seaside. It was always a whole fish she desired, not shellfish, or the fillets Eliot's mother had broiled one night a few months ago when she'd invited a man from her office to dinner — a man who'd spent the night in his mother's bedroom, but whom Eliot never saw again. One evening when Eliot's mother came to pick him up, Mrs. Sen served her a tuna croquette, explaining that it was really supposed to be made with a fish called bhetki. "It is very frustrating," Mrs. Sen apologized, with an emphasis on the second syllable of the word. "To live so close to the ocean and not to have so much fish." In the summer, she said, she liked to go to a market by the beach. She added that while the fish there tasted nothing like the fish in India, at least it was fresh. Now that it was getting colder, the boats were no longer going out regularly, and sometimes there was no whole fish available for weeks at a time.

"Try the supermarket," his mother suggested.

Mrs. Sen shook her head. "In the supermarket I can feed a cat thirty-two dinners from one of thirty-two tins, but I can never find a single fish I like, never a single." Mrs. Sen said she had grown up eating fish twice a day. She added that in Calcutta people ate fish first thing in the morning, last thing before bed, as a snack after school if they were lucky. They ate the tail, the eggs, even the head. It was available in any market, at any hour, from dawn until midnight. "All you have to do is leave the house and walk a bit, and there you are."

Every few days Mrs. Sen would open up the yellow pages, dial a number that she had ticked in the margin, and ask if there was any whole fish available. If so, she would ask the market to hold it. "Under Sen, yes, S as in Sam, N as in New York. Mr. Sen will be there to pick it up." Then she would call Mr. Sen at the university. A few minutes later Mr. Sen would arrive, patting Eliot on the head but not kissing Mrs. Sen. He read his mail at the Formica table and drank a cup of tea before heading out; half an hour later he would return, carrying a paper bag with a smiling lobster drawn on the front of it, and hand it to Mrs. Sen, and head back to the university to teach his evening class. One day, when he handed Mrs. Sen the paper bag, he said, "No more fish for a while. Cook the chicken in the freezer. I need to start holding office hours."

For the next few days, instead of calling the fish market, Mrs. Sen thawed chicken legs in the kitchen sink and chopped them with her blade. One day she made a stew with green beans and tinned sardines. But the following week the man who ran the fish market called Mrs. Sen; he assumed she wanted the fish, and said he would hold it until the end of the day under her name. She was flattered. "Isn't that nice of him, Eliot? The man said he looked up my name in the telephone book. He said there is only one Sen. Do you know how many Sens are in the Calcutta telephone book?"

She told Eliot to put on his shoes and his jacket, and then she called Mr. Sen at the university. Eliot tied his sneakers by the bookcase and waited for her to join him, to choose from her row of slippers. After a few minutes he called out her name. When Mrs. Sen did not reply, he untied his sneakers and returned to the living room, where he found her on the sofa, weeping. Her face was in her hands and tears dripped through her fingers. Through them she murmured something about a meeting Mr. Sen was required to attend. Slowly she stood up and rearranged the cloth over the telephone. Eliot followed her, walking for the first time in his sneakers across the pear-colored carpet. She stared at him. Her lower eyelids were swollen into thin pink crests. "Tell me, Eliot. Is it too much to ask?"

Before he could answer, she took him by the hand and led him to the bedroom, whose door was normally kept shut. Apart from the bed, which lacked a headboard, the only other things in the room were a side table with a telephone on it, an ironing board, and a bureau. She flung open the drawers of the bureau and the door of the closet, filled with saris of every imaginable texture and shade, brocaded with gold and silver threads. Some were transparent, tissue thin, others as thick as drapes, with tassels knotted along the edges. In the closet they were on hangers; in the drawers they were folded flat, or wound tightly like thick scrolls. She sifted through the drawers, letting saris spill over the edges. "When have I ever worn this one? And this? And this?" She tossed the saris one by one from the drawers, then pried several from their hangers. They landed like a pile of tangled sheets on the bed. The room was filled with an intense smell of mothballs.

"'Send pictures,' they write. 'Send pictures of your new life.' What picture can I send?" She sat, exhausted, on the edge of the bed, where there was now barely room for her. "They think I live the life of a queen, Eliot." She looked around the blank walls of the room. "They think I press buttons and the house is clean. They think I live in a palace."

The phone rang. Mrs. Sen let it ring several times before

picking up the extension by the bed. During the conversation she seemed only to be replying to things, and wiping her face with the ends of one of the saris. When she got off the phone she stuffed the saris without folding them back into the drawers, and then she and Eliot put on their shoes and went to the car, where they waited for Mr. Sen to meet them.

"Why don't you drive today?" Mr. Sen asked when he appeared, rapping on the hood of the car with his knuckles. They always spoke to each other in English when Eliot was present.

"Not today. Another day."

"How do you expect to pass the test if you refuse to drive on a road with other cars?"

"Eliot is here today."

"He is here every day. It's for your own good. Eliot, tell Mrs. Sen it's for her own good."

She refused.

They drove in silence, along the same roads that Eliot and his mother took back to the beach house each evening. But in the back seat of Mr. and Mrs. Sen's car the ride seemed unfamiliar, and took longer than usual. The gulls whose tedious cries woke him each morning now thrilled him as they dipped and flapped across the sky. They passed one beach after another, and the shacks, now locked up, that sold frozen lemonade and quahogs in summer. Only one of the shacks was open. It was the fish market.

Mrs. Sen unlocked her door and turned toward Mr. Sen, who had not yet unfastened his seat belt. "Are you coming?"

Mr. Sen handed her some bills from his wallet. "I have a meeting in twenty minutes," he said, staring at the dashboard as he spoke. "Please don't waste time."

Eliot accompanied her into the dank little shop, whose walls were festooned with nets and starfish and buoys. A group of tourists with cameras around their necks huddled by the counter, some sampling stuffed clams, others pointing to a large chart illustrating fifty different varieties of North Atlantic fish. Mrs. Sen took a ticket from the machine at the counter and waited in line. Eliot stood by the lobsters, which stirred one on top of another in their murky tank, their claws bound by yellow rubber bands. He watched as Mrs. Sen laughed and chatted, when it was her turn in line, with a man with a bright red face and yellow teeth, dressed in a black rubber apron. In either hand he held a mackerel by the tail.

"You are sure what you sell me is very fresh?"

"Any fresher and they'd answer that question themselves."

The dial shivered toward its verdict on the scale.

"You want this cleaned, Mrs. Sen?"

She nodded. "Leave the heads on, please."

"You got cats at home?"

"No cats. Only a husband."

Later, in the apartment, she pulled the blade out of the cupboard, spread newspapers across the carpet, and inspected her treasures. One by one she drew them from the paper wrapping, wrinkled and tinged with blood. She stroked the tails, prodded the bellies, pried apart the gutted flesh. With a pair of scissors she clipped the fins. She tucked a finger under the gills, a red so bright they made her vermilion seem pale. She grasped the body, lined with inky streaks, at either end, and notched it at intervals against the blade.

"Why do you do that?" Eliot asked.

"To see how many pieces. If I cut properly, from this fish I will get three meals." She sawed off the head and set it on a pie plate.

In November came a series of days when Mrs. Sen refused to practice driving. The blade never emerged from the cupboard, newspapers were not spread on the floor. She did not call the fish store, nor did she thaw chicken. In silence she prepared crackers with peanut butter for Eliot, then sat reading old aerograms from a shoebox. When it was time for Eliot to leave she gathered together his things without inviting his mother to sit on the sofa and eat something first. When, eventually, his mother asked him in the car if he'd noticed a change in Mrs. Sen's behavior, he said he hadn't. He didn't tell her that Mrs. Sen paced the apartment, staring at the plastic-covered lampshades as if noticing them for the first time. He didn't tell her she switched on the television but never watched it, or that she made herself tea but let it grow cold on the coffee table. One day she played a tape of something she called a raga; it sounded a little bit like someone plucking very slowly and then very quickly on a violin, and Mrs. Sen said it was supposed to be heard only in the late afternoon, as the sun was setting. As the music played, for nearly an hour, she sat on the sofa with her eyes closed. Afterward she said, "It is more sad even than your Beethoven, isn't it?" Another day she played a cassette of people talking in her language — a farewell present, she told Eliot, that her family had made for her. As the succession of voices laughed and said their bit, Mrs. Sen identified each speaker. "My third uncle, my cousin, my father, my grandfather." One speaker sang a song. Another recited a poem. The final voice on the tape belonged to Mrs. Sen's mother. It was quieter and sounded more serious than the others. There was a pause between each sentence, and during this pause Mrs. Sen translated for Eliot: "The price of goat rose two rupees. The mangoes at the market are not very sweet. College Street is flooded." She turned off the tape. "These are things that happened the day I left India." The next day she played the same cassette all over again. This time, when her grandfather was speaking, she stopped the tape. She told Eliot she'd received a letter over the weekend. Her grand-father was dead.

A week later Mrs. Sen began cooking again. One day as she sat slicing cabbage on the living room floor, Mr. Sen called. He wanted to take Eliot and Mrs. Sen to the seaside. For the occasion Mrs. Sen put on a red sari and red lipstick; she fresh-ened the vermilion in her part and rebraided her hair. She knotted a scarf under her chin, arranged her sunglasses on top of her head, and put a pocket camera in her purse. As Mr. Sen backed out of the parking lot, he put his arm across the top of the front seat, so that it looked as if he had his arm around Mrs. Sen. "It's getting too cold for that top coat," he said to her at one point. "We should get you something warmer." At the shop they bought mackerel, and butterfish, and sea bass. This time Mr. Sen came into the shop with them. It was Mr. Sen who asked whether the fish was fresh and to cut it this way or that way. They bought so much fish that Eliot had to hold one of the bags. After they put the bags in the trunk, Mr. Sen announced that he was hungry, and Mrs. Sen agreed, so they crossed the street to a restaurant where the take-out win-dow was still open. They sat at a picnic table and ate two bas-kets of clam cakes. Mrs. Sen put a good deal of Tabasco sauce and black pepper on hers. "Like pakoras, no?" Her face was flushed, her lipstick faded, and she laughed at everything Mr. Sen said.

Behind the restaurant was a small beach, and when they were done eating they walked for a while along the shore, into a wind so strong that they had to walk backward. Mrs. Sen pointed to the water, and said that at a certain moment, each wave resembled a sari drying on a clothesline. "Impossible!" she shouted eventually, laughing as she turned back, her eyes teary. "I cannot move." Instead she took a picture of Eliot and Mr. Sen standing on the sand. "Now one of us," she said, pressing Eliot against her checkered coat and giving the camera to Mr. Sen. Finally the camera was given to Eliot. "Hold it steady," said Mr. Sen. Eliot looked through the tiny window in the camera and waited for Mr. and Mrs. Sen to move closer together, but they didn't. They didn't hold hands or put their arms around each other's waists. Both smiled with their mouths closed, squinting into the wind, Mrs. Sen's red sari leaping like flames under her coat.

In the car, warm at last and exhausted from the wind and the clam cakes, they admired the dunes, the ships they could see in the distance, the view of the lighthouse, the peach and purple sky. After a while Mr. Sen slowed down and stopped by the side of the road.

"What's wrong?" Mrs. Sen asked.

"You are going to drive home today."

"Not today."

"Yes, today." Mr. Sen stepped out of the car and opened the door on Mrs. Sen's side. A fierce wind blew into the car, accompanied by the sound of waves crashing on the shore. Finally she slid over to the driver's side, but spent a long time adjusting her sari and her sunglasses. Eliot turned and looked through the back window. The road was empty. Mrs. Sen turned on the radio, filling up the car with violin music.

"There's no need," Mr. Sen said, clicking it off.

"It helps me to concentrate," Mrs. Sen said, and turned the radio on again.

"Put on your signal," Mr. Sen directed.

"I know what to do."

For about a mile she was fine, though far slower than the other cars that passed her. But when the town approached, and traffic lights loomed on wires in the distance, she went even slower.

"Switch lanes," Mr. Sen said. "You will have to bear left at the rotary."

Mrs. Sen did not.

"Switch lanes, I tell you." He shut off the radio. "Are you listening to me?"

A car beeped its horn, then another. She beeped defiantly in response, stopped, then pulled without signaling to the side of the road. "No more," she said, her forehead resting against the top of the steering wheel. "I hate it. I hate driving. I won't go on."

She stopped driving after that. The next time the fish store called she did not call Mr. Sen at his office. She had decided to try something new. There was a town bus that ran on an hourly schedule between the university and the seaside. After the university it made two stops, first at a nursing home, then at a shopping plaza without a name, which consisted of a bookstore, a shoe store, a drugstore, a pet store, and a record store. On benches under the portico, elderly women from the nursing home sat in pairs, in knee-length overcoats with over-sized buttons, eating lozenges.

"Eliot," Mrs. Sen asked him while they were sitting on the bus, "will you put your mother in a nursing home when she is old?"

"Maybe," he said. "But I would visit every day."

"You say that now, but you will see, when you are a man your life will be in places you cannot know now." She counted on her fingers: "You will have a wife, and children of your own, and they will want to be driven to different places at the same time. No matter how kind they are, one day they will complain about visiting your mother, and you will get tired of it too, Eliot. You will miss one day, and another, and then she will have to drag herself onto a bus just to get herself a bag of lozenges."

At the fish shop the ice beds were nearly empty, as were the lobster tanks, where rust-colored stains were visible through the water. A sign said the shop would be closing for winter at the end of the month. There was only one person working behind the counter, a young boy who did not recognize Mrs. Sen as he handed her a bag reserved under her name.

"Has it been cleaned and scaled?" Mrs. Sen asked.

The boy shrugged. "My boss left early. He just said to give you this bag."

In the parking lot Mrs. Sen consulted the bus schedule. They would have to wait forty-five minutes for the next one, and so they crossed the street and bought clam cakes at the take-out window they had been to before. There was no place to sit. The picnic tables were no longer in use, their benches chained upside down on top of them.

On the way home an old woman on the bus kept watching them, her eyes shifting from Mrs. Sen to Eliot to the blood-lined bag between their feet. She wore a black overcoat, and in her lap she held, with gnarled, colorless hands, a crisp white bag from the drugstore. The only other passengers were two college students, boyfriend and girlfriend, wearing matching sweatshirts, their fingers linked, slouched in the back seat. In silence Eliot and Mrs. Sen ate the last few clam cakes in the bag. Mrs. Sen had forgotten napkins, and traces of fried batter dotted the corners of her mouth. When they reached the nursing home the woman in the overcoat stood up, said something to the driver, then stepped off the bus. The driver turned his head and glanced back at Mrs. Sen. "What's in the bag?"

Mrs. Sen looked up, startled.

"Speak English?" The bus began to move again, causing the driver to look at Mrs. Sen and Eliot in his enormous rearview mirror.

"Yes, I can speak."

"Then what's in the bag?"

"A fish," Mrs. Sen replied.

"The smell seems to be bothering the other passengers. Kid, maybe you should open her window or something."

One afternoon a few days later the phone rang. Some very tasty halibut had arrived on the boats. Would Mrs. Sen like to pick one up? She called Mr. Sen, but he was not at his desk. A second time she tried calling, then a third. Eventually she went to the kitchen and returned to the living room with the blade, an eggplant, and some newspapers. Without having to be told Eliot took his place on the sofa and watched as she sliced the stems off the eggplant. She divided it into long, slender strips, then into small squares, smaller and smaller, as small as sugar cubes.

"I am going to put these in a very tasty stew with fish and green bananas," she announced. "Only I will have to do without the green bananas."

"Are we going to get the fish?"

"We are going to get the fish."

"Is Mr. Sen going to take us?"

"Put on your shoes."

They left the apartment without cleaning up. Outside it was so cold that Eliot could feel the chill on his teeth. They got in the car, and Mrs. Sen drove around the asphalt loop several times. Each time she paused by the grove of pine trees to observe the traffic on the main road. Eliot thought she was just practicing while they waited for Mr. Sen. But then she gave a signal and turned.

The accident occurred quickly. After about a mile Mrs. Sen took a left before she should have, and though the oncoming car managed to swerve out of her way, she was so startled by the horn that she lost control of the wheel and hit a telephone pole on the opposite corner. A policeman arrived and asked to see her license, but she did not have one to show him. "Mr. Sen teaches mathematics at the university" was all she said by way of explanation.

The damage was slight. Mrs. Sen cut her lip, Eliot complained briefly of a pain in his ribs, and the car's fender would have to be straightened. The policeman thought Mrs. Sen had also cut her scalp, but it was only the vermilion. When Mr. Sen arrived, driven by one of his colleagues, he spoke at length with the policeman as he filled out some forms, but he said nothing to Mrs. Sen as he drove them back to the apartment. When they got out of the car, Mr. Sen patted Eliot's head. "The policeman said you were lucky. Very lucky to come out without a scratch."

After taking off her slippers and putting them on the bookcase, Mrs. Sen put away the blade that was still on the living room floor and threw the eggplant pieces and the newspapers into the garbage pail. She prepared a plate of crackers with peanut butter, placed them on the coffee table, and turned on the television for Eliot's benefit. "If he is still hungry give him a Popsicle from the box in the freezer," she said to Mr. Sen, who sat at the Formica table sorting through the mail. Then she went into her bedroom and shut the door. When Eliot's mother arrived at quarter to six, Mr. Sen told her the details of the accident and offered a check reimbursing November's payment. As he wrote out the check he apologized on behalf of

Mrs. Sen. He said she was resting, though when Eliot had gone to the bathroom he'd heard her crying. His mother was satisfied with the arrangement, and in a sense, she confessed to Eliot as they drove home, she was relieved. It was the last afternoon Eliot spent with Mrs. Sen, or with any baby-sitter. From then on his mother gave him a key, which he wore on a string around his neck. He was to call the neighbors in case of an emergency, and to let himself into the beach house after school. The first day, just as he was taking off his coat, the phone rang. It was his mother calling from her office. "You're a big boy now, Eliot," she told him. "You okay?" Eliot looked out the kitchen window, at gray waves receding from the shore, and said that he was fine.

This Blessed House

T HEY DISCOVERED the first one in a cupboard above the stove, beside an unopened bottle of malt vinegar.

"Guess what I found." Twinkle walked into the living room, lined from end to end with taped-up packing boxes, waving the vinegar in one hand and a white porcelain effigy of Christ, roughly the same size as the vinegar bottle, in the other.

Sanjeev looked up. He was kneeling on the floor, marking, with ripped bits of a Post-it, patches on the baseboard that needed to be retouched with paint. "Throw it away."

"Which?"

"Both."

"But I can cook something with the vinegar. It's brand-new."

"You've never cooked anything with vinegar."

"I'll look something up. In one of those books we got for our wedding."

Sanjeev turned back to the baseboard, to replace a Post-it scrap that had fallen to the floor. "Check the expiration. And at the very least get rid of that idiotic statue."

"But it could be worth something. Who knows?" She turned

it upside down, then stroked, with her index finger, the minuscule frozen folds of its robes. "It's pretty."

"We're not Christian," Sanjeev said. Lately he had begun noticing the need to state the obvious to Twinkle. The day before he had to tell her that if she dragged her end of the bureau instead of lifting it, the parquet floor would scratch.

She shrugged. "No, we're not Christian. We're good little Hindus." She planted a kiss on top of Christ's head, then placed the statue on top of the fireplace mantel, which needed, Sanjeev observed, to be dusted.

By the end of the week the mantel had still not been dusted; it had, however, come to serve as the display shelf for a sizable collection of Christian paraphernalia. There was a 3-D postcard of Saint Francis done in four colors, which Twinkle had found taped to the back of the medicine cabinet, and a wooden cross key chain, which Sanjeev had stepped on with bare feet as he was installing extra shelving in Twinkle's study. There was a framed paint-by-number of the three wise men, against a black velvet background, tucked in the linen closet. There was also a tile trivet depicting a blond, unbearded Jesus, delivering a sermon on a mountaintop, left in one of the drawers of the built-in china cabinet in the dining room.

"Do you think the previous owners were born-agains?" asked Twinkle, making room the next day for a small plastic snow-filled dome containing a miniature Nativity scene, found behind the pipes of the kitchen sink.

Sanjeev was organizing his engineering texts from MIT in alphabetical order on a bookshelf, though it had been several years since he had needed to consult any of them. After graduating, he moved from Boston to Connecticut, to work for a firm near Hartford, and he had recently learned that he was being considered for the position of vice president. At thirty-three he had a secretary of his own and a dozen people working under his supervision who gladly supplied him with any information he needed. Still, the presence of his college books in the room reminded him of a time in his life he recalled with fondness, when he would walk each evening across the Mass. Avenue bridge to order Mughlai chicken with spinach from his favorite Indian restaurant on the other side of the Charles, and return to his dorm to write out clean copies of his problem sets.

"Or perhaps it's an attempt to convert people," Twinkle mused.

"Clearly the scheme has succeeded in your case."

She disregarded him, shaking the little plastic dome so that the snow swirled over the manger.

He studied the items on the mantel. It puzzled him that each was in its own way so silly. Clearly they lacked a sense of sacredness. He was further puzzled that Twinkle, who normally displayed good taste, was so charmed. These objects meant something to Twinkle, but they meant nothing to him. They irritated him. "We should call the Realtor. Tell him there's all this nonsense left behind. Tell him to take it away."

"Oh, Sanj." Twinkle groaned. "Please. I would feel terrible throwing them away. Obviously they were important to the people who used to live here. It would feel, I don't know, sacrilegious or something."

"If they're so precious, then why are they hidden all over the house? Why didn't they take them with them?

"There must be others," Twinkle said. Her eyes roamed the bare off-white walls of the room, as if there were other things concealed behind the plaster. "What else do you think we'll find?"

But as they unpacked their boxes and hung up their winter clothes and the silk paintings of elephant processions bought on their honeymoon in Jaipur, Twinkle, much to her dismay, could not find a thing. Nearly a week had passed before they discovered, one Saturday afternoon, a larger-than-life-sized watercolor poster of Christ, weeping translucent tears the size of peanut shells and sporting a crown of thorns, rolled up behind a radiator in the guest bedroom. Sanjeev had mistaken it for a window shade.

"Oh, we must, we simply must put it up. It's too spectacular." Twinkle lit a cigarette and began to smoke it with relish, waving it around Sanjeev's head as if it were a conductor's baton as Mahler's Fifth Symphony roared from the stereo downstairs.

"Now, look. I will tolerate, for now, your little biblical menagerie in the living room. But I refuse to have this," he said, flicking at one of the painted peanut-tears, "displayed in our home."

Twinkle stared at him, placidly exhaling, the smoke emerging in two thin blue streams from her nostrils. She rolled up the poster slowly, securing it with one of the elastic bands she always wore around her wrist for tying back her thick, unruly hair, streaked here and there with henna. "I'm going to put it in my study," she informed him. "That way you don't have to look at it."

"What about the housewarming? They'll want to see all the rooms. I've invited people from the office."

She rolled her eyes. Sanjeev noted that the symphony, now in its third movement, had reached a crescendo, for it pulsed with the telltale clashing of cymbals.

"I'll put it behind the door," she offered. "That way, when they peek in, they won't see. Happy?"

He stood watching her as she left the room, with her poster and her cigarette; a few ashes had fallen to the floor where she'd been standing. He bent down, pinched them between his fingers, and deposited them in his cupped palm. The tender fourth movement, the *adagietto,* began. During breakfast, Sanjeev had read in the liner notes that Mahler had proposed to his wife by sending her the manuscript of this portion of the score. Although there were elements of tragedy and struggle in the Fifth Symphony, he had read, it was principally music of love and happiness.

He heard the toilet flush. "By the way," Twinkle hollered, "if you want to impress people, I wouldn't play this music. It's putting me to sleep."

Sanjeev went to the bathroom to throw away the ashes. The cigarette butt still bobbed in the toilet bowl, but the tank was refilling, so he had to wait a moment before he could flush it again. In the mirror of the medicine cabinet he inspected his long eyelashes — like a girl's, Twinkle liked to tease. Though he was of average build, his cheeks had a plumpness to them; this, along with the eyelashes, detracted, he feared, from what he hoped was a distinguished profile. He was of average height as well, and had wished ever since he had stopped growing that he were just one inch taller. For this reason it irritated him when Twinkle insisted on wearing high heels, as she had done the other night when they ate dinner in Manhattan. This was the first weekend after they'd moved into the house; by then the mantel had already filled up considerably, and they had bickered about it in the car on the way down. But then Twinkle had drunk four glasses of whiskey in a nameless bar in Alphabet City, and forgot all about it. She dragged him to a tiny bookshop on St. Mark's Place, where she browsed for nearly an hour, and when they left she insisted that they dance a tango on the sidewalk in front of strangers.

Afterward, she tottered on his arm, rising faintly over his line of vision, in a pair of suede three-inch leopard-print pumps. In this manner they walked the endless blocks back to a parking garage on Washington Square, for Sanjeev had heard far too many stories about the terrible things that happened to cars in Manhattan. "But I do nothing all day except sit at my desk," she fretted when they were driving home, after he had mentioned that her shoes looked uncomfortable and suggested that perhaps she should not wear them. "I can't exactly wear heels when I'm typing." Though he abandoned the argument, he knew for a fact that she didn't spend all day at her desk; just that afternoon, when he got back from a run, he found her inexplicably in bed, reading. When he asked why she was in bed in the middle of the day she told him she was bored. He had wanted to say to her then, You could unpack some boxes. You could sweep the attic. You could retouch the paint on the bathroom windowsill, and after you do it you could warn me so that I don't put my watch on it. They didn't bother her, these scattered, unsettled matters. She seemed content with whatever clothes she found at the front of the closet, with whatever magazine was lying around, with whatever song was on the radio — content yet curious. And now all of her curiosity centered around discovering the next treasure.

A few days later when Sanjeev returned from the office, he found Twinkle on the telephone, smoking and talking to one of her girlfriends in California even though it was before five o'clock and the long-distance rates were at their peak. "Highly devout people," she was saying, pausing every now and then to exhale. "Each day is like a treasure hunt. I'm serious. This you won't believe. The switch plates in the bedrooms were decorated with scenes from the Bible. You know, Noah's Ark and all that. Three bedrooms, but one is my study. Sanjeev went to the hardware store right away and replaced them, can you imagine, he replaced every single one."

Now it was the friend's turn to talk. Twinkle nodded, slouched on the floor in front of the fridge, wearing black stirrup pants and a yellow chenille sweater, groping for her lighter. Sanjeev could smell something aromatic on the stove, and he picked his way carefully across the extra-long phone cord tangled on the Mexican terra-cotta tiles. He opened the lid of a pot with some sort of reddish brown sauce dripping over the sides, boiling furiously.

"It's a stew made with fish. I put the vinegar in it," she said to him, interrupting her friend, crossing her fingers. "Sorry, you were saying?" She was like that, excited and delighted by little things, crossing her fingers before any remotely unpredictable event, like tasting a new flavor of ice cream, or dropping a letter in a mailbox. It was a quality he did not understand. It made him feel stupid, as if the world contained hidden wonders he could not anticipate, or see. He looked at her face, which, it occurred to him, had not grown out of its girlhood, the eyes untroubled, the pleasing features unfirm, as if they still had to settle into some sort of permanent expression. Nicknamed after a nursery rhyme, she had yet to shed a childhood endearment. Now, in the second month of their marriage, certain things nettled him — the way she sometimes spat a little when she spoke, or left her undergarments after removing them at night at the foot of their bed rather than depositing them in the laundry hamper.

They had met only four months before. Her parents, who lived in California, and his, who still lived in Calcutta, were old friends, and across continents they had arranged the occasion at which Twinkle and Sanjeev were introduced — a sixteenth birthday party for a daughter in their circle — when Sanjeev was in Palo Alto on business. At the restaurant they were seated side by side at a round table with a revolving platter of spareribs and egg rolls and chicken wings, which, they concurred, all tasted the same. They had concurred too on their adolescent but still persistent fondness for Wodehouse novels, and their dislike for the sitar, and later Twinkle confessed that she was charmed by the way Sanjeev had dutifully refilled her teacup during their conversation.

And so the phone calls began, and grew longer, and then the visits, first he to Stanford, then she to Connecticut, after which Sanjeev would save in an ashtray left on the balcony the crushed cigarettes she had smoked during the weekend — saved them, that is, until the next time she came to visit him, and then he vacuumed the apartment, washed the sheets, even dusted the plant leaves in her honor. She was twenty-seven and recently abandoned, he had gathered, by an American who had tried and failed to be an actor; Sanjeev was lonely, with an excessively generous income for a single man, and had never been in love. At the urging of their matchmakers, they married in India, amid hundreds of well-wishers whom he barely remembered from his childhood, in incessant August rains, under a red and orange tent strung with Christmas tree lights on Mandeville Road.

"Did you sweep the attic?" he asked Twinkle later as she was folding paper napkins and wedging them by their plates. The attic was the only part of the house they had not yet given an initial cleaning.

"Not yet. I will, I promise. I hope this tastes good," she said, planting the steaming pot on top of the Jesus trivet. There was a loaf of Italian bread in a little basket, and iceberg lettuce and grated carrots tossed with bottled dressing and croutons, and glasses of red wine. She was not terribly ambitious in the kitchen. She bought preroasted chickens from the supermarket and served them with potato salad prepared who knew when, sold in little plastic containers. Indian food, she complained, was a bother; she detested chopping garlic, and peeling ginger, and could not operate a blender, and so it was Sanjeev who, on weekends, seasoned mustard oil with cinnamon sticks and cloves in order to produce a proper curry.

He had to admit, though, that whatever it was that she had cooked today, it was unusually tasty, attractive even, with bright white cubes of fish, and flecks of parsley, and fresh tomatoes gleaming in the dark brown-red broth.

"How did you make it?"

"I made it up."

"What did you do?"

"I just put some things into the pot and added the malt vinegar at the end."

"How much vinegar?"

She shrugged, ripping off some bread and plunging it into her bowl.

"What do you mean you don't know? You should write it down. What if you need to make it again, for a party or something?"

"I'll remember," she said. She covered the bread basket with a dishtowel that had, he suddenly noticed, the Ten Commandments printed on it. She flashed him a smile, giving his knee a little squeeze under the table. "Face it. This house is blessed."

The housewarming party was scheduled for the last Saturday in October, and they had invited about thirty people. All were Sanjeev's acquaintances, people from the office, and a number of Indian couples in the Connecticut area, many of whom he barely knew, but who had regularly invited him, in his bachelor days, to supper on Saturdays. He often wondered why they included him in their circle. He had little in common with any of them, but he always attended their gatherings, to eat spiced chickpeas and shrimp cutlets, and gossip and discuss politics, for he seldom had other plans. So far, no one had met Twinkle; back when they were still dating, Sanjeev didn't want to waste their brief weekends together with people he associated with being alone. Other than Sanjeev and an ex-boyfriend who she believed worked in a pottery studio in Brookfield, she knew no one in the state of Connecticut. She was completing her master's thesis at Stanford, a study of an Irish poet whom Sanjeev had never heard of.

Sanjeev had found the house on his own before leaving for the wedding, for a good price, in a neighborhood with a fine school system. He was impressed by the elegant curved staircase with its wrought-iron banister, and the dark wooden wainscoting, and the solarium overlooking rhododendron bushes, and the solid brass 22, which also happened to be the date of his birth, nailed impressively to the vaguely Tudor facade. There were two working fireplaces, a two-car garage, and an attic suitable for converting into extra bedrooms if, the Realtor mentioned, the need should arise. By then Sanjeev had already made up his mind, was determined that he and Twinkle should live there together, forever, and so he had not bothered to notice the switch plates covered with biblical stickers, or the transparent decal of the Virgin on the half shell, as Twinkle liked to call it, adhered to the window in the master bedroom. When, after moving in, he tried to scrape it off, he scratched the glass.

The weekend before the party they were raking the lawn when he heard Twinkle shriek. He ran to her, clutching his rake, worried that she had discovered a dead animal, or a snake. A brisk October breeze stung the tops of his ears as his sneakers crunched over brown and yellow leaves. When he reached her, she had collapsed on the grass, dissolved in nearly silent laughter. Behind an overgrown forsythia bush was a plaster Virgin Mary as tall as their waists, with a blue painted hood draped over her head in the manner of an Indian bride. Twinkle grabbed the hem of her T-shirt and began wiping away the dirt staining the statue's brow.

"I suppose you want to put her by the foot of our bed," Sanjeev said.

She looked at him, astonished. Her belly was exposed, and he saw that there were goose bumps around her navel. "What do you think? Of course we can't put this in our bedroom."

"We can't?"

"No, silly Sanj. This is meant for outside. For the lawn."

"Oh God, no. Twinkle, no."

"But we must. It would be bad luck not to."

"All the neighbors will see. They'll think we're insane."

"Why, for having a statue of the Virgin Mary on our lawn? Every other person in this neighborhood has a statue of Mary on the lawn. We'll fit right in."

"We're not Christian."

"So you keep reminding me." She spat onto the tip of her finger and started to rub intently at a particularly stubborn stain on Mary's chin. "Do you think this is dirt, or some kind of fungus?"

He was getting nowhere with her, with this woman whom he had known for only four months and whom he had married, this woman with whom he now shared his life. He thought with a flicker of regret of the snapshots his mother used to send him from Calcutta, of prospective brides who could sing and sew and season lentils without consulting a cookbook. Sanjeev had considered these women, had even ranked them in order of preference, but then he had met

Twinkle. "Twinkle, I can't have the people I work with see this statue on my lawn."

"They can't fire you for being a believer. It would be discrimination."

"That's not the point."

"Why does it matter to you so much what other people think?"

"Twinkle, please." He was tired. He let his weight rest against his rake as she began dragging the statue toward an oval bed of myrtle, beside the lamppost that flanked the brick pathway. "Look, Sanj. She's so lovely."

He returned to his pile of leaves and began to deposit them by handfuls into a plastic garbage bag. Over his head the blue sky was cloudless. One tree on the lawn was still full of leaves, red and orange, like the tent in which he had married Twinkle.

He did not know if he loved her. He said he did when she had first asked him, one afternoon in Palo Alto as they sat side by side in a darkened, nearly empty movie theater. Before the film, one of her favorites, something in German that he found extremely depressing, she had pressed the tip of her nose to his so that he could feel the flutter of her mascara-coated eyelashes. That afternoon he had replied, yes, he loved her, and she was delighted, and fed him a piece of popcorn, letting her finger linger an instant between his lips, as if it were his reward for coming up with the right answer.

Though she did not say it herself, he assumed then that she loved him too, but now he was no longer sure. In truth, Sanjeev did not know what love was, only what he thought it was not. It was not, he had decided, returning to an empty carpeted condominium each night, and using only the top fork in his cutlery drawer, and turning away politely at those weekend dinner parties when the other men eventually put their arms around the waists of their wives and girlfriends, leaning over every now and again to kiss their shoulders or necks. It was not sending away for classical music CDs by mail, working his way methodically through the major composers that the catalogue recommended, and always sending his payments in on time. In the months before meeting Twinkle, Sanjeev had begun to realize this. "You have enough money in the bank to raise three families," his mother reminded him when they spoke at the start of each month on the phone. "You need a wife to look after and love." Now he had one, a pretty one, from a suitably high caste, who would soon have a master's degree. What was there not to love?

That evening Sanjeev poured himself a gin and tonic, drank it and most of another during one segment of the news, and then approached Twinkle, who was taking a bubble bath, for she announced that her limbs ached from raking the lawn, something she had never done before. He didn't knock. She had applied a bright blue mask to her face, was smoking and sipping some bourbon with ice and leafing through a fat paperback book whose pages had buckled and turned gray from the water. He glanced at the cover; the only thing written on it was the word "Sonnets" in dark red letters. He took a breath, and then he informed her very calmly that after finishing his drink he was going to put on his shoes and go outside and remove the Virgin from the front lawn.

"Where are you going to put it?" she asked him dreamily, her eyes closed. One of her legs emerged, unfolding gracefully, from the layer of suds. She flexed and pointed her toes.

"For now I am going to put it in the garage. Then tomorrow morning on my way to work I am going to take it to the dump."

"Don't you dare." She stood up, letting the book fall into the water, bubbles dripping down her thighs. "I hate you," she informed him, her eyes narrowing at the word "hate." She reached for her bathrobe, tied it tightly about her waist, and padded down the winding staircase, leaving sloppy wet footprints along the parquet floor. When she reached the foyer, Sanjeev said, "Are you planning on leaving the house that way?" He felt a throbbing in his temples, and his voice revealed an unfamiliar snarl when he spoke.

"Who cares? Who cares what way I leave this house?"

"Where are you planning on going at this hour?"

"You can't throw away that statue. I won't let you." Her mask, now dry, had assumed an ashen quality, and water from her hair dripped onto the caked contours of her face.

"Yes I can. I will."

"No," Twinkle said, her voice suddenly small. "This is our house. We own it together. The statue is a part of our property." She had begun to shiver. A small pool of bathwater had collected around her ankles. He went to shut a window, fearing that she would catch cold. Then he noticed that some of the water dripping down her hard blue face was tears.

"Oh God, Twinkle, please, I didn't mean it." He had never seen her cry before, had never seen such sadness in her eyes. She didn't turn away or try to stop the tears; instead she looked strangely at peace. For a moment she closed her lids, pale and unprotected compared to the blue that caked the rest of her face. Sanjeev felt ill, as if he had eaten either too much or too little.

She went to him, placing her damp toweled arms about his neck, sobbing into his chest, soaking his shirt. The mask flaked onto his shoulders.

In the end they settled on a compromise: the statue would be placed in a recess at the side of the house, so that it wasn't obvious to passersby, but was still clearly visible to all who came.

The menu for the party was fairly simple: there would be a case of champagne, and samosas from an Indian restaurant in Hartford, and big trays of rice with chicken and almonds and orange peels, which Sanjeev had spent the greater part of the morning and afternoon preparing. He had never entertained on such a large scale before and, worried that there would not be enough to drink, ran out at one point to buy another case of champagne just in case. For this reason he burned one of the rice trays and had to start it over again. Twinkle swept the floors and volunteered to pick up the samosas; she had an appointment for a manicure and a pedicure in that direction, anyway. Sanjeev had planned to ask if she would consider clearing the menagerie off the mantel, if only for the party, but she left while he was in the shower. She was gone for a good three hours, and so it was Sanjeev who did the rest of the cleaning. By five-thirty the entire house sparkled, with scented candles that Twinkle had picked up in Hartford illuminating the items on the mantel, and slender stalks of burning incense planted into the soil of potted plants. Each time he passed the mantel he winced, dreading the raised eyebrows of his guests as they viewed the flickering ceramic saints, the salt and pepper shakers designed to resemble Mary and Joseph. Still, they would be impressed, he hoped, by the lovely bay windows, the shining parquet floors, the impressive winding staircase, the wooden wainscoting, as they sipped champagne and dipped samosas in chutney.

Douglas, one of the new consultants at the firm, and his girlfriend Nora were the first to arrive. Both were tall and blond, wearing matching wire-rimmed glasses and long black overcoats. Nora wore a black hat full of sharp thin feathers that corresponded to the sharp thin angles of her face. Her left hand was joined with Douglas's. In her right hand was a bottle of cognac with a red ribbon wrapped around its neck, which she gave to Twinkle.

"Great lawn, Sanjeev," Douglas remarked. "We've got to get that rake out ourselves, sweetie. And this must be . . ."

"My wife. Tanima."

"Call me Twinkle."

"What an unusual name," Nora remarked.

Twinkle shrugged. "Not really. There's an actress in Bombay named Dimple Kapadia. She even has a sister named Simple."

Douglas and Nora raised their eyebrows simultaneously, nodding slowly, as if to let the absurdity of the names settle in. "Pleased to meet you, Twinkle."

"Help yourself to champagne. There's gallons."

"I hope you don't mind my asking," Douglas said, "but I noticed the statue outside, and are you guys Christian? I thought you were Indian."

"There are Christians in India," Sanjeev replied, "but we're not."

"I love your outfit," Nora told Twinkle.

"And I adore your hat. Would you like the grand tour?"

The bell rang again, and again and again. Within minutes, it seemed, the house had filled with bodies and conversations and unfamiliar fragrances. The women wore heels and sheer stockings, and short black dresses made of crepe and chiffon. They handed their wraps and coats to Sanjeev, who draped them carefully on hangers in the spacious coat closet, though Twinkle told people to throw their things on the ottomans in the solarium. Some of the Indian women wore their finest saris, made with gold filigree that draped in elegant pleats over their shoulders. The men wore jackets and ties and citrus-scented aftershaves. As people filtered from one room to the next, presents piled onto the long cherry-wood table that ran from one end of the downstairs hall to the other.

It bewildered Sanjeev that it was for him, and his house, and his wife, that they had all gone to so much care. The only other time in his life that something similar had happened was his wedding day, but somehow this was different, for these were not his family, but people who knew him only casually, and in a sense owed him nothing. Everyone congratulated him. Lester, another coworker, predicted that Sanjeev would be promoted to vice president in two months maximum. People devoured the samosas, and dutifully admired the freshly painted ceilings and walls, the hanging plants, the bay windows, the silk paintings from Jaipur. But most of all they admired Twinkle, and her brocaded *salwar-kameez*, which was the shade of a persimmon with a low scoop in the back, and the little string of white rose petals she had coiled cleverly around her head, and the pearl choker with a sapphire at its center that adorned her throat. Over hectic jazz records, played under Twinkle's supervision, they laughed at her anecdotes and observations, forming a widening circle around her, while Sanjeev replenished the samosas that he kept warming evenly in the oven, and getting ice for people's drinks, and opening more bottles of champagne with some difficulty, and explaining for the fortieth time that he wasn't Christian. It was Twinkle who led them in separate groups up and down the winding stairs, to gaze at the back lawn, to peer down the cellar steps. "Your friends adore the poster in my study," she mentioned to him triumphantly, placing her hand on the small of his back as they, at one point, brushed past each other.

Sanjeev went to the kitchen, which was empty, and ate a piece of chicken out of the tray on the counter with his fingers because he thought no one was looking. He ate a second piece, then washed it down with a gulp of gin straight from the bottle.

"Great house. Great rice." Sunil, an anesthesiologist, walked in, spooning food from his paper plate into his mouth. "Do you have more champagne?"

"Your wife's wow," added Prabal, following behind. He was an unmarried professor of physics at Yale. For a moment Sanjeev stared at him blankly, then blushed; once at a dinner party Prabal had pronounced that Sophia Loren was wow, as was Audrey Hepburn. "Does she have a sister?"

Sunil picked a raisin out of the rice tray. "Is her last name Little Star?"

The two men laughed and started eating more rice from the tray, plowing through it with their plastic spoons. Sanjeev went down to the cellar for more liquor. For a few minutes he paused on the steps, in the damp, cool silence, hugging the second crate of champagne to his chest as the party drifted above the rafters. Then he set the reinforcements on the dining table.

"Yes, everything, we found them all in the house, in the most unusual places," he heard Twinkle saying in the living room. "In fact we keep finding them."

"No!"

"Yes! Every day is like a treasure hunt. It's too good. God only knows what else we'll find, no pun intended."

That was what started it. As if by some unspoken pact, the whole party joined forces and began combing through each of the rooms, opening closets on their own, peering under chairs and cushions, feeling behind curtains, removing books from bookcases. Groups scampered, giggling and swaying, up and down the winding staircase.

"We've never explored the attic," Twinkle announced suddenly, and so everybody followed.

"How do we get up there?"

"There's a ladder in the hallway, somewhere in the ceiling."

Wearily Sanjeev followed at the back of the crowd, to point out the location of the ladder, but Twinkle had already found it on her own. "Eureka!" she hollered.

Douglas pulled the chain that released the steps. His face was flushed and he was wearing Nora's feather hat on his head. One by one the guests disappeared, men helping women as they placed their strappy high heels on the narrow slats of the ladder, the Indian women wrapping the free ends of their expensive saris into their waistbands. The men followed behind, all quickly disappearing, until Sanjeev alone remained at the top of the winding staircase. Footsteps thundered over his head. He had no desire to join them. He wondered if the ceiling would collapse, imagined, for a split second, the sight of all the tumbling drunk perfumed bodies crashing, tangled, around him. He heard a shriek, and then rising, spreading waves of laughter in discordant tones. Something fell, something else shattered. He could hear them babbling about a trunk. They seemed to be struggling to get it open, banging feverishly on its surface.

He thought perhaps Twinkle would call for his assistance, but he was not summoned. He looked about the hallway and to the landing below, at the champagne glasses and half-eaten samosas and napkins smeared with lipstick abandoned in every corner, on every available surface. Then he noticed that Twinkle, in her haste, had discarded her shoes altogether, for they lay by the foot of the ladder, black patent-leather mules with heels like golf tees, open toes, and slightly soiled silk labels on the instep where her soles had rested. He placed them in the doorway of the master bedroom so that no one would trip when they descended.

He heard something creaking open slowly. The strident voices had subsided to an even murmur. It occurred to Sanjeev that he had the house all to himself. The music had ended and he could hear, if he concentrated, the hum of the refrigerator, and the rustle of the last leaves on the trees outside, and the tapping of their branches against the windowpanes. With one flick of his hand he could snap the ladder back on its spring into the ceiling, and they would have no way of getting down unless he were to pull the chain and let them. He thought of all the things he could do, undisturbed. He could sweep Twinkle's menagerie into a garbage bag and get in the car and drive it all to the dump, and tear down the poster of weeping Jesus, and take a hammer to the Virgin Mary while he was at it. Then he would return to the empty house; he could easily clear up the cups and plates in an hour's time, and pour himself a gin and tonic, and eat a plate of warmed rice and listen to his new Bach CD while reading the liner notes so as to understand it properly. He nudged the ladder slightly, but it was sturdily planted against the floor. Budging it would require some effort.

"My God, I need a cigarette," Twinkle exclaimed from above.

Sanjeev felt knots forming at the back of his neck. He felt dizzy. He needed to lie down. He walked toward the bedroom, but stopped short when he saw Twinkle's shoes facing him in the doorway. He thought of her slipping them on her feet. But instead of feeling irritated, as he had ever since they'd moved into the house together, he felt a pang of anticipation at the thought of her rushing unsteadily down the winding staircase in them, scratching the floor a bit in her path. The pang intensified as he thought of her rushing to the bathroom to brighten her lipstick, and eventually rushing to get people their coats, and finally rushing to the cherry-wood table when the last guest had left, to begin opening their housewarming presents. It was the same pang he used to feel before they were married, when he would hang up the phone after one of their conversations, or when he would drive back from the airport, wondering which ascending plane in the sky was hers.

"Sanj, you won't believe this."

She emerged with her back to him, her hands over her head, the tops of her bare shoulder blades perspiring, supporting something still hidden from view.

"You got it, Twinkle?" someone asked.

"Yes, you can let go."

Now he saw that her hands were wrapped around it: a solid silver bust of Christ, the head easily three times the size of his own. It had a patrician bump on its nose, magnificent curly hair that rested atop a pronounced collarbone, and a broad forehead that reflected in miniature the walls and doors and lampshades around them. Its expression was confident, as if assured of its devotees, the unyielding lips sensuous and full. It was also sporting Nora's feather hat. As Twinkle descended, Sanjeev put his hands around her waist to balance her, and he relieved her of the bust when she had reached the ground. It weighed a good thirty pounds. The others began lowering themselves slowly, exhausted from the hunt. Some trickled downstairs in search of a fresh drink.

She took a breath, raised her eyebrows, crossed her fingers. "Would you mind terribly if we displayed it on the mantel? Just for tonight? I know you hate it."

He did hate it. He hated its immensity, and its flawless, polished surface, and its undeniable value. He hated that it was in his house, and that he owned it. Unlike the other things they'd found, this contained dignity, solemnity, beauty even. But to his surprise these qualities made him hate it all the more. Most of all he hated it because he knew that Twinkle loved it.

"I'll keep it in my study from tomorrow," Twinkle added. "I promise."

She would never put it in her study, he knew. For the rest of their days together she would keep it on the center of the mantel, flanked on either side by the rest of the menagerie. Each time they had guests Twinkle would explain how she had found it, and they would admire her as they listened. He gazed at the crushed rose petals in her hair, at the pearl and sapphire choker at her throat, at the sparkly crimson polish on her toes. He decided these were among the things that made Prabal think she was wow. His head ached from gin and his arms ached from the weight of the statue. He said, "I put your shoes in the bedroom."

"Thanks. But my feet are killing me." Twinkle gave his elbow a little squeeze and headed for the living room.

Sanjeev pressed the massive silver face to his ribs, careful not to let the feather hat slip, and followed her.

The Treatment
of Bibi Haldar

FOR THE GREATER NUMBER of her twenty-nine years, Bibi Haldar suffered from an ailment that baffled family, friends, priests, palmists, spinsters, gem therapists, prophets, and fools. In efforts to cure her, concerned members of our town brought her holy water from seven holy rivers. When we heard her screams and throes in the night, when her wrists were bound with ropes and stinging poultices pressed upon her, we named her in our prayers. Wise men had massaged eucalyptus balm into her temples, steamed her face with herbal infusions. At the suggestion of a blind Christian she was once taken by train to kiss the tombs of saints and martyrs. Amulets warding against the evil eye girded her arms and neck. Auspicious stones adorned her fingers.

Treatments offered by doctors only made matters worse. Allopaths, homeopaths, ayurvedics — over time, all branches of the medical arts had been consulted. Their advice was endless. After x-rays, probes, auscultations, and injections, some merely advised Bibi to gain weight, others to lose it. If one forbade her to sleep beyond dawn, another insisted she remain in bed till noon. This one told her to perform headstands, that one to chant Vedic verses at specified intervals throughout the day. "Take her to Calcutta for hypnosis" was a suggestion still others would offer. Shuttled from one specialist to the next, the girl had been prescribed to shun garlic, consume disproportionate quantities of bitters, meditate, drink green coconut water, and swallow raw duck's eggs beaten in milk. In short, Bibi's life was an encounter with one fruitless antidote after another.

The nature of her illness, which struck without warning, confined her world to the unpainted four-story building in which her only local family, an elder cousin and his wife, rented an apartment on the second floor. Liable to fall unconscious and enter, at any moment, into a shameless delirium, Bibi could be trusted neither to cross a street nor board a tram without supervision. Her daily occupation consisted of sitting in the storage room on the roof of our building, a space in which one could sit but not comfortably stand, featuring an adjoining latrine, a curtained entrance, one window without a grille, and shelves made from the panels of old doors. There, cross-legged on a square of jute, she recorded inventory for the cosmetics shop that her cousin Haldar owned and managed at the mouth of our courtyard. For her services, Bibi received no income but was given meals, provisions, and sufficient meters of cotton at every October holiday to replenish her wardrobe at an inexpensive tailor. At night she slept on a folding camp cot in the cousin's place downstairs.

In the mornings Bibi arrived in the storage room wearing cracked plastic slippers and a housecoat whose hem stopped some inches below the knee, a length we had not worn since we were fifteen. Her shins were hairless, and sprayed with a generous number of pallid freckles. She bemoaned her fate and challenged her stars as we hung our laundry or scrubbed scales from our fish. She was not pretty. Her upper lip was thin, her teeth too small. Her gums protruded when she spoke. "I ask you, is it fair for a girl to sit out her years, pass neglected through her prime, listing labels and prices without promise of a future?" Her voice was louder than necessary, as if she were speaking to a deaf person. "Is it wrong to envy you, all brides and mothers, busy with lives and cares? Wrong to want to shade my eyes, scent my hair? To raise a child and teach him sweet from sour, good from bad?"

Each day she unloaded her countless privations upon us, until it became unendurably apparent that Bibi wanted a man. She wanted to be spoken for, protected, placed on her path in life. Like the rest of us, she wanted to serve suppers, and scold servants, and set aside money in her *almari* to have her eyebrows threaded every three weeks at the Chinese beauty parlor. She pestered us for details of our own weddings: the jewels, the invitations, the scent of tuberoses strung over the nuptial bed. When, at her insistence, we showed her our photo albums embossed with the designs of butterflies, she pored over the snapshots that chronicled the ceremony: butter poured in fires, garlands exchanged, vermilion-painted fish, trays of shells and silver coins. "An impressive number of guests," she would observe, stroking with her finger the misplaced faces that had surrounded us. "When it happens to me, you will all be present."

Anticipation began to plague her with such ferocity that the thought of a husband, on which all her hopes were pinned, threatened at times to send her into another attack. Amid tins of talc and boxes of bobby pins she would curl up on the floor of the storage room, speaking in non sequiturs. "I will never dip my feet in milk," she whimpered. "My face will never be painted with sandalwood paste. Who will rub me with turmeric? My name will never be printed with scarlet ink on a card."

Her soliloquies mawkish, her sentiments maudlin, malaise dripped like a fever from her pores. In her most embittered moments we wrapped her in shawls, washed her face from the cistern tap, and brought her glasses of yogurt and rosewater. In moments when she was less disconsolate, we encouraged her to accompany us to the tailor and replenish her blouses and petticoats, in part to provide her with a change of scenery, and in part because we thought it might increase whatever matrimonial prospects she had. "No man wants a woman who dresses like a dishwasher," we told her. "Do you want all that fabric of yours to go to the moths?" She sulked, pouted, protested, and sighed. "Where do I go, who would I dress for?" she demanded. "Who takes me to the cinema, the zoo-garden, buys me lime soda and cashews? Admit it, are these concerns of mine? I will never be cured, never married."

But then a new treatment was prescribed for Bibi, the most outrageous of them all. One evening on her way to dinner, she collapsed on the third-floor landing, pounding her fists, kicking her feet, sweating buckets, lost to this world. Her moans echoed through the stairwell, and we rushed out of our apartments to calm her at once, bearing palm fans and sugar cubes, and tumblers of refrigerated water to pour on her head. Our children clung to the banisters and witnessed her paroxysm; our servants were sent to summon her cousin. It was ten minutes before Haldar emerged from his shop, impassive apart from the red in his face. He told us to stop fussing, and then with no efforts to repress his disdain he packed her into a rickshaw bound for the polyclinic. It was there, after performing a series of blood tests, that the doctor in charge of Bibi's case, exasperated, concluded that a marriage would cure her.

News spread between our window bars, across our clothes-lines, and over the pigeon droppings that plastered the parapets of our rooftops. By the next morning, three separate palmists had examined Bibi's hand and confirmed that there was, no doubt, evidence of an imminent union etched into her skin. Unsavory sorts murmured indelicacies at cutlet stands; grandmothers consulted almanacs to determine a propitious hour for the betrothal. For days afterward, as we walked our children to school, picked up our cleaning, stood in lines at the ration shop, we whispered. Apparently some activity was what the poor girl needed all along. For the first time we imagined the contours below her housecoat, and attempted to appraise the pleasures she could offer a man. For the first time we noted the clarity of her complexion, the length and languor of her eyelashes, the undeniably elegant armature of her hands. "They say it's the only hope. A case of overexcitement. They say" — and here we paused, blushing — "relations will calm her blood."

Needless to say, Bibi was delighted by the diagnosis, and began at once to prepare for conjugal life. With some damaged merchandise from Haldar's shop she polished her toenails and softened her elbows. Neglecting the new shipments delivered to the storage room, she began hounding us for recipes, for vermicelli pudding and papaya stew, and inscribed them in crooked letters in the pages of her inventory ledger. She made guest lists, dessert lists, listed lands in which she intended to honeymoon. She applied glycerine to smooth her lips, resisted sweets to reduce her measurements. One day she asked one of us to accompany her to the tailor, who stitched her a new *salwar-kameez* in an umbrella cut, the fashion that season. On the streets she dragged us to the counters of each and every jeweler, peering into glass cases, seeking our opinions of tiara designs and locket settings. In the windows of sari shops she pointed to a magenta Benarasi silk, and a turquoise one, and then one that was the color of marigolds. "The first part of the ceremony I will wear this one, then this one, then this."

But Haldar and his wife thought otherwise. Immune to her fancies, indifferent to our fears, they conducted business as usual, stuffed together in that cosmetics shop no bigger than a wardrobe, whose walls were crammed on three sides with hennas, hair oils, pumice stones, and fairness creams. "We have little time for indecent suggestions," replied Haldar to those who broached the subject of Bibi's health. "What won't be cured must be endured. Bibi has caused enough worry, added enough to expenses, sullied enough the family name." His wife, seated beside him behind the tiny glass counter, fanned the mottled skin above her breasts and agreed. She was a heavy woman whose powder, a shade too pale for her, caked in the creases of her throat. "Besides, who would marry her? The girl knows nothing about anything, speaks backward, is practically thirty, can't light a coal stove, can't boil rice, can't tell the difference between fennel and a cumin seed. Imagine her attempting to feed a man!"

They had a point. Bibi had never been taught to be a woman; the illness had left her naive in most practical matters. Haldar's wife, convinced that the devil himself possessed her, kept Bibi away from fire and flame. She had not been taught to wear a sari without pinning it in four different places, nor could she embroider slipcovers or crochet shawls with any exceptional talent. She was not allowed to watch the television (Haldar assumed its electronic properties would excite her), and was thus ignorant of the events and entertainments of our world. Her formal studies had ended after the ninth standard.

For Bibi's sake we argued in favor of finding a husband. "It's what she's wanted all along," we pointed out. But Haldar and his wife were impossible to reason with. Their rancor toward Bibi was fixed on their lips, thinner than the strings with which they tied our purchases. When we maintained that the new treatment deserved a chance, they contended, "Bibi possesses insufficient quantities of respect and self-control. She plays up her malady for the attention. The best thing is to keep her occupied, away from the trouble she invariably creates."

"Why not marry her off, then? It will get her off your hands, at least."

"And waste our profits on a wedding? Feeding guests, ordering bracelets, buying a bed, assembling a dowry?"

But Bibi's gripes persisted. Late one morning, dressed under our supervision in a sari of lavender eyelet chiffon and mirrored slippers lent to her for the occasion, she hastened in uneven steps to Haldar's shop and insisted on being taken to the photographer's studio so that her portrait, like those of other brides-in-waiting, could be circulated in the homes of eligible men. Through the shutters of our balconies we watched her; perspiration had already left black moons beneath her armpits. "Apart from my x-rays I have never been photographed," she fretted. "Potential in-laws need to know what I look like." But Haldar refused. He said that anyone who wished to see her could observe her for themselves, weeping and wailing and warding off customers. She was a bane for business, he told her, a liability and a loss. Who in this town needed a photo to know that?

The next day Bibi stopped listing inventory altogether and regaled us, instead, with imprudent details about Haldar and his wife. "On Sundays he plucks hairs from her chin. They keep their money refrigerated under lock and key." For the benefit of neighboring rooftops she strutted and shrieked; with each proclamation her audience expanded. "In the bath she applies chickpea flour to her arms because she thinks it will make her paler. The third toe on her right foot is missing. The reason they take such long siestas is that she is impossible to please."

To get her to quiet down, Haldar placed a one-line advertisement in the town newspaper, in order to solicit a groom: "GIRL, UNSTABLE, HEIGHT 152 CENTIMETRES, SEEKS HUSBAND." The identity of the prospective bride was no secret to the parents of our young men, and no family was willing to shoulder so blatant a risk. Who could blame them? It was rumored by many that Bibi conversed with herself in a fluent but totally incomprehensible language, and slept without dreams. Even the lonely four-toothed widower who repaired our handbags in the market could not be persuaded to propose. Nevertheless, to distract her, we began to coach her in wifely ways. "Frowning like a rice pot will get you nowhere. Men require that you caress them with your expression." As practice for the event of encountering a possible suitor, we urged her to engage in small conversations with nearby men. When the water bearer arrived, at the end of his rounds, to fill Bibi's urn in the storage room, we instructed her to say "How do you do?" When the coal supplier unloaded his baskets on the roof, we advised her to smile and make a comment about the weather. Recalling our own experiences, we prepared her for an interview. "Most likely the groom will arrive with one parent, a grandparent, and either an uncle or aunt. They will stare, ask several questions. They will examine the bottoms of your feet, the thickness of your braid. They will ask you to name the prime minister, recite poetry, feed a dozen hungry people on half a dozen eggs."

When two months had passed without a single reply to the

advertisement, Haldar and his wife felt vindicated. "Now do you see that she is unfit to marry? Now do you see no man of sane mind would touch her?"

Things had not been so bad for Bibi before her father died. (The mother had not survived beyond the birth of the girl.) In his final years, the old man, a teacher of mathematics in our elementary schools, had kept assiduous track of Bibi's illness in hopes of determining some logic to her condition. "To every problem there is a solution," he would reply whenever we inquired after his progress. He reassured Bibi. For a time he reassured us all. He wrote letters to doctors in England, spent his evenings reading casebooks at the library, gave up eating meat on Fridays in order to appease his household god. Eventually he gave up teaching as well, tutoring only from his room, so that he could monitor Bibi at all hours. But though in his youth he had received prizes for his ability to deduce square roots from memory, he was unable to solve the mystery of his daughter's disease. For all his work, his records led him to conclude only that Bibi's attacks occurred more frequently in summer than winter, and that she had suffered approximately twenty-five major attacks in all. He created a chart of her symptoms with directions for calming her, and distributed it throughout the neighborhood, but these were eventually lost, or turned into sailboats by our children, or used to calculate grocery budgets on the reverse side.

Apart from keeping her company, apart from soothing her woes, apart from keeping an occasional eye on her, there was little we could do to improve the situation. None of us were capable of understanding such desolation. Some days, after siesta, we combed out her hair, remembering now and then to change the part in her scalp so that it would not grow too broad. At her request we powdered the down over her lips and throat, penciled definition into her brows, and walked her to the banks of the fish pond where our children played cricket in the afternoon. She was still determined to lure a man.

"Apart from my condition I am perfectly healthy," she maintained, seating herself on a bench along the footpath where courting men and women strolled hand in hand. "I have never had a cold or flu. I have never had jaundice. I have never suffered from colic or indigestion." Sometimes we bought her smoked corn on the cob sprinkled with lemon juice, or two *paisa* caramels. We consoled her; when she was convinced a man was giving her the eye, we humored her and agreed. But she was not our responsibility, and in our private moments we were thankful for it.

In November we learned that Haldar's wife was pregnant. That morning in the storage room, Bibi wept. "She says I'm contagious, like the pox. She says I'll spoil the baby." She was breathing heavily, her pupils fixed to a peeling spot on the wall. "What will become of me?" There was still no response to the advertisement in the newspaper. "Is it not punishment enough that I bear this curse alone? Must I also be blamed for infecting another?" Dissent within the Haldar household grew. The wife, convinced that Bibi's presence would infect the unborn child, began to wrap woolen shawls around her tumid belly. In the bathroom Bibi was given separate soaps and towels. According to the scullery maid, Bibi's plates were not washed with the others.

And then one afternoon, without word or warning, it happened again. On the banks of the fish pond, Bibi fell to the footpath. She shook. She shuddered. She chewed her lips. A group encircled the convulsing girl at once, eager to assist in whatever way possible. The opener of soda bottles pinned down her thrashing limbs. The vendor of sliced cucumbers attempted to unclasp her fingers. One of us doused her with

water from the pond. Another wiped her mouth with a perfumed handkerchief. The seller of jackfruits was holding Bibi's
head, which struggled to toss from side to side. And the man
who cranked the sugarcane press gripped the palm fan that he
ordinarily used to chase away flies, agitating the air from every
conceivable angle.

"Is there a doctor in the crowd?"

"Watch that she doesn't swallow her tongue."

"Has anyone informed Haldar?"

"She's hotter than coals!"

In spite of our efforts, the tumult persisted. Wrestling with
her adversary, wracked with anguish, she ground her teeth
and twitched at the knees. Over two minutes had passed. We
watched and worried. We wondered what to do.

"Leather!" someone cried suddenly. "She needs to smell
leather." Then we remembered; the last time it had happened,
a cowhide sandal held under her nostrils was what had finally
freed Bibi from the clutches of her torment.

"Bibi, what happened? Tell us what happened," we asked
when she opened her eyes.

"I felt hot, then hotter. Smoke passed before my eyes. The
world went black. Didn't you see it?"

A group of our husbands escorted her home. Dusk thick-
ened, conch shells were blown, and the air grew dense with the
incense of prayers. Bibi muttered and staggered but said nothing. Her cheeks were bruised and nicked here and there. Her
hair was matted, her elbows caked with dirt, and a small piece
of one front tooth was missing. We followed behind, at what
we assumed to be safe distances, holding our children by the
hand.

She needed a blanket, a compress, a sedative tablet. She
needed supervision. But when we reached the courtyard Haldar and his wife would not have her in the flat.

"The medical risk is too great for an expectant mother to be in contact with an hysterical person," he insisted.

That night Bibi slept in the storage room.

Their baby, a girl, was delivered by forceps at the end of June. By then Bibi was sleeping downstairs again, though they kept her camp cot in the corridor, and would not let her touch the child directly. Every day they sent her to the roof to record inventory until lunch, at which point Haldar brought her receipts from the morning's sales and a bowl of yellow split peas for her lunch. At night she ate milk and bread alone in the stairwell. Another seizure, and another, went unchecked.

When we voiced our concern, Haldar said it was not our business, and flatly refused to discuss the matter. To express our indignation we began to take our shopping elsewhere; this provided us with our only revenge. Over the weeks the products on Haldar's shelves grew dusty. Labels faded and colognes turned rank. Passing by in the evenings, we saw Haldar sitting alone, swatting moths with the sole of his slipper. We hardly saw the wife at all. According to the scullery maid she was still bedridden; apparently her labor had been complicated.

Autumn came, with its promise of the October holidays, and the town grew busy shopping and planning for the season. Film songs blared from amplifiers strung through trees. Arcades and markets stayed open all hours. We bought our children balloons and colored ribbons, purchased sweetmeats by the kilo, paid calls in taxis to relatives we had not seen throughout the year. The days grew shorter, the evenings colder. We buttoned our sweaters and pulled up our socks. Then a chill set in that made our throats itch. We made our children gargle with warm saltwater and wrap mufflers around their necks. But it was the Haldar baby who ended up getting sick.

A doctor was summoned in the middle of the night and

commanded to reduce the fever. "Cure her," the wife pleaded. Her shrill commotion had woken us all. "We can give you anything, just cure my baby girl." The doctor prescribed a glucose formula, crushed aspirins in a mortar, and told them to wrap the child with quilts and covers.

Five days later the fever had not budged.

"It's Bibi," the wife wailed. "She's done it, she's infected our child. We should never have let her back down here. We should never have let her back into this house."

And so Bibi started to spend her nights in the storage room again. At the wife's insistence Haldar even moved her camp cot up there, along with a tin trunk that contained her belongings. Her meals were left covered with a colander at the top of the stairs.

"I don't mind," Bibi told us. "It's better to live apart from them, to set up house on my own." She unpacked the trunk — some housecoats, a framed portrait of her father, sewing supplies, and an assortment of fabrics — and arranged her things on a few empty shelves. By the week's end the baby had recuperated, but Bibi was not asked to return downstairs. "Don't worry, it's not as if they've locked me in here," she said in order to set us at ease. "The world begins at the bottom of the stairs. Now I am free to discover life as I please."

But in truth she stopped going out altogether. When we asked her to come with us to the fish pond or to go see temple decorations she refused, claiming that she was stitching a new curtain to hang across the entrance of the storage room. Her skin looked ashen. She needed fresh air. "What about finding your husband?" we suggested. "How do you expect to charm a man sitting up here all day?"

Nothing persuaded her.

*   *   *

By mid-December, Haldar cleared all the unsold merchandise off the shelves of his beauty shop and hauled them in boxes up to the storage room. We had succeeded in driving him more or less out of business. Before the year's end the family moved away, leaving an envelope containing three hundred rupees under Bibi's door. There was no more news of them.

One of us had an address for a relation of Bibi's in Hydera-bad, and wrote explaining the situation. The letter was re-turned unopened, address unknown. Before the coldest weeks set in, we had the shutters of the storage room repaired and attached a sheet of tin to the doorframe, so that she would at least have some privacy. Someone donated a kerosene lamp; another gave her some old mosquito netting and a pair of socks without heels. At every opportunity we reminded her that we surrounded her, that she could come to us if she ever needed advice or aid of any kind. For a time we sent our children to play on the roof in the afternoons, so that they could alert us if she was having another attack. But each night we left her alone.

Some months passed. Bibi had retreated into a deep and prolonged silence. We took turns leaving her plates of rice and glasses of tea. She drank little, ate less, and began to assume an expression that no longer matched her years. At twilight she circled the parapet once or twice, but she never left the rooftop. After dark she remained behind the tin door and did not come out for any reason. We did not disturb her. Some of us began to wonder if she was dying. Others concluded that she had lost her mind.

One morning in April, when the heat had returned for dry-ing lentil wafers on the roof, we noticed that someone had vomited by the cistern tap. When we noticed this a second morning as well, we knocked on Bibi's tin door. When there was no answer we opened it ourselves, as there was no lock to fasten it.

We found her lying on the camp cot. She was about four months pregnant.

She said she could not remember what had happened. She would not tell us who had done it. We prepared her semolina with hot milk and raisins; still she would not reveal the man's identity. In vain we searched for traces of the assault, some sign of the intrusion, but the room was swept and in order. On the floor beside the cot, her inventory ledger, open to a fresh page, contained a list of names.

She carried the baby to full term, and one evening in September, we helped her deliver a son. We showed her how to feed him, and bathe him, and lull him to sleep. We bought her an oilcloth and helped her stitch clothes and pillowcases out of the fabric she had saved over the years. Within a month Bibi had recuperated from the birth, and with the money that Haldar had left her, she had the storage room white-washed, and placed padlocks on the window and doors. Then she dusted the shelves and arranged the leftover potions and lotions, selling Haldar's old inventory at half price. She told us to spread word of the sale, and we did. From Bibi we purchased our soaps and kohl, our combs and powders, and when she had sold the last of her merchandise, she went by taxi to the wholesale market, using her profits to restock the shelves. In this manner she raised the boy and ran a business in the storage room, and we did what we could to help. For years afterward, we wondered who in our town had disgraced her. A few of our servants were questioned, and in tea stalls and bus stands, possible suspects were debated and dismissed. But there was no point carrying out an investigation. She was, to the best of our knowledge, cured.

The Third and
Final Continent

I LEFT INDIA IN 1964 with a certificate in commerce and the equivalent, in those days, of ten dollars to my name. For three weeks I sailed on the SS *Roma,* an Italian cargo vessel, in a third-class cabin next to the ship's engine, across the Arabian Sea, the Red Sea, the Mediterranean, and finally to England. I lived in north London, in Finsbury Park, in a house occupied entirely by penniless Bengali bachelors like myself, at least a dozen and sometimes more, all struggling to educate and establish ourselves abroad.

I attended lectures at LSE and worked at the university library to get by. We lived three or four to a room, shared a single, icy toilet, and took turns cooking pots of egg curry, which we ate with our hands on a table covered with newspapers. Apart from our jobs we had few responsibilities. On weekends we lounged barefoot in drawstring pajamas, drinking tea and smoking Rothmans, or set out to watch cricket at Lord's. Some weekends the house was crammed with still more Bengalis, to whom we had introduced ourselves at the greengrocer, or on the Tube, and we made yet more egg curry, and played Mukhesh on a Grundig reel-to-reel, and soaked our dirty dishes in the bathtub. Every now and then someone in the house moved out, to live with a woman whom his family back in Calcutta had determined he was to wed. In 1969, when I was thirty-six years old, my own marriage was arranged. Around the same time I was offered a full-time job in America, in the processing department of a library at MIT. The salary was generous enough to support a wife, and I was honored to be hired by a world-famous university, and so I obtained a sixth-preference green card, and prepared to travel farther still.

By now I had enough money to go by plane. I flew first to Calcutta, to attend my wedding, and a week later I flew to Boston, to begin my new job. During the flight I read *The Student Guide to North America*, a paperback volume that I'd bought before leaving London, for seven shillings six pence on Tottenham Court Road, for although I was no longer a student I was on a budget all the same. I learned that Americans drove on the right side of the road, not the left, and that they called a lift an elevator and an engaged phone busy. "The pace of life in North America is different from Britain as you will soon discover," the guidebook informed me. "Everybody feels he must get to the top. Don't expect an English cup of tea." As the plane began its descent over Boston Harbor, the pilot announced the weather and time, and that President Nixon had declared a national holiday: two American men had landed on the moon. Several passengers cheered. "God bless America!" one of them hollered. Across the aisle, I saw a woman praying.

I spent my first night at the YMCA in Central Square, Cambridge, an inexpensive accommodation recommended by my guidebook. It was walking distance from MIT, and steps from the post office and a supermarket called Purity Supreme. The room contained a cot, a desk, and a small wooden cross on one wall. A sign on the door said cooking was strictly forbidden. A bare window overlooked Massachusetts Avenue, a major thoroughfare with traffic in both directions. Car horns, shrill and prolonged, blared one after another. Flashing sirens heralded endless emergencies, and a fleet of buses rumbled past, their doors opening and closing with a powerful hiss, throughout the night. The noise was constantly distracting, at times suffocating. I felt it deep in my ribs, just as I had felt the furious drone of the engine on the SS *Roma*. But there was no ship's deck to escape to, no glittering ocean to thrill my soul, no breeze to cool my face, no one to talk to. I was too tired to pace the gloomy corridors of the YMCA in my drawstring pajamas. Instead I sat at the desk and stared out the window, at the city hall of Cambridge and a row of small shops. In the morning I reported to my job at the Dewey Library, a beige fortlike building by Memorial Drive. I also opened a bank account, rented a post office box, and bought a plastic bowl and a spoon at Woolworth's, a store whose name I recognized from London. I went to Purity Supreme, wandering up and down the aisles, converting ounces to grams and comparing prices to things in England. In the end I bought a small carton of milk and a box of cornflakes. This was my first meal in America. I ate it at my desk. I preferred it to hamburgers or hot dogs, the only alternative I could afford in the coffee shops on Massachusetts Avenue, and, besides, at the time I had yet to consume any beef. Even the simple chore of buying milk was new to me; in London we'd had bottles delivered each morning to our door.

In a week I had adjusted, more or less. I ate cornflakes and milk, morning and night, and bought some bananas for variety, slicing them into the bowl with the edge of my spoon. In addition I bought tea bags and a flask, which the salesman in Woolworth's referred to as a thermos (a flask, he informed me, was used to store whiskey, another thing I had never consumed). For the price of one cup of tea at a coffee shop, I filled the flask with boiling water on my way to work each morning, and brewed the four cups I drank in the course of a day. I bought a larger carton of milk, and learned to leave it on the shaded part of the windowsill, as I had seen another resident at the YMCA do. To pass the time in the evenings I read the *Boston Globe* downstairs, in a spacious room with stained-glass windows. I read every article and advertisement, so that I would grow familiar with things, and when my eyes grew tired I slept. Only I did not sleep well. Each night I had to keep the window wide open; it was the only source of air in the stifling room, and the noise was intolerable. I would lie on the cot with my fingers pressed into my ears, but when I drifted off to sleep my hands fell away, and the noise of the traffic would wake me up again. Pigeon feathers drifted onto the windowsill, and one evening, when I poured milk over my cornflakes, I saw that it had soured. Nevertheless I resolved to stay at the YMCA for six weeks, until my wife's passport and green card were ready. Once she arrived I would have to rent a proper apartment, and from time to time I studied the classified section of the newspaper, or stopped in at the housing office at MIT during my lunch break, to see what was available in my price range. It was in this manner that I discovered a room for immediate occupancy, in a house on a quiet street, the listing said, for eight dollars per week. I copied the number into my guidebook and dialed from a pay telephone, sorting through the coins with which I was still unfamiliar, smaller and lighter than shillings, heavier and brighter than *paisas*.

"Who is speaking?" a woman demanded. Her voice was bold and clamorous.

"Yes, good afternoon, madame. I am calling about the room for rent."

"Harvard or Tech?"

"I beg your pardon?"

"Are you from Harvard or Tech?"

Gathering that Tech referred to the Massachusetts Institute of Technology, I replied, "I work at Dewey Library," adding tentatively, "at Tech."

"I only rent rooms to boys from Harvard or Tech!"

"Yes, madame."

I was given an address and an appointment for seven o'clock that evening. Thirty minutes before the hour I set out, my guidebook in my pocket, my breath fresh with Listerine. I turned down a street shaded with trees, perpendicular to Massachusetts Avenue. Stray blades of grass poked between the cracks of the footpath. In spite of the heat I wore a coat and a tie, regarding the event as I would any other interview; I had never lived in the home of a person who was not Indian. The house, surrounded by a chain-link fence, was off-white with dark brown trim. Unlike the stucco row house I'd lived in in London, this house, fully detached, was covered with wooden shingles, with a tangle of forsythia bushes plastered against the front and sides. When I pressed the calling bell, the woman with whom I had spoken on the phone hollered from what seemed to be just the other side of the door, "One minute, please!"

Several minutes later the door was opened by a tiny, extremely old woman. A mass of snowy hair was arranged like a small sack on top of her head. As I stepped into the house she sat down on a wooden bench positioned at the bottom of a narrow carpeted staircase. Once she was settled on the bench, in a small pool of light, she peered up at me with undivided attention. She wore a long black skirt that spread like a stiff tent to the floor, and a starched white shirt edged with ruffles at the throat and cuffs. Her hands, folded together in her lap, had long pallid fingers, with swollen knuckles and tough yellow nails. Age had battered her features so that she almost resembled a man, with sharp, shrunken eyes and prominent creases on either side of her nose. Her lips, chapped and faded, had nearly disappeared, and her eyebrows were missing altogether. Nevertheless she looked fierce.

"Lock up!" she commanded. She shouted even though I stood only a few feet away. "Fasten the chain and firmly press that button on the knob! This is the first thing you shall do when you enter, is that clear?"

I locked the door as directed and examined the house. Next to the bench on which the woman sat was a small round table, its legs fully concealed, much like the woman's, by a skirt of lace. The table held a lamp, a transistor radio, a leather change purse with a silver clasp, and a telephone. A thick wooden cane coated with a layer of dust was propped against one side. There was a parlor to my right, lined with bookcases and filled with shabby claw-footed furniture. In the corner of the parlor I saw a grand piano with its top down, piled with papers. The piano's bench was missing; it seemed to be the one on which the woman was sitting. Somewhere in the house a clock chimed seven times.

"You're punctual!" the woman proclaimed. "I expect you shall be so with the rent!"

"I have a letter, madame." In my jacket pocket was a letter confirming my employment from MIT, which I had brought along to prove that I was indeed from Tech.

She stared at the letter, then handed it back to me carefully, gripping it with her fingers as if it were a dinner plate heaped with food instead of a sheet of paper. She did not wear glasses, and I wondered if she'd read a word of it. "The last boy was always late! Still owes me eight dollars! Harvard boys aren't what they used to be! Only Harvard and Tech in this house! How's Tech, boy?"

"It is very well."

"You checked the lock?"

"Yes, madame."

She slapped the space beside her on the bench with one hand, and told me to sit down. For a moment she was silent. Then she intoned, as if she alone possessed this knowledge:

"There is an American flag on the moon!"

"Yes, madame." Until then I had not thought very much about the moon shot. It was in the newspaper, of course, article upon article. The astronauts had landed on the shores of the Sea of Tranquillity, I had read, traveling farther than anyone in the history of civilization. For a few hours they explored the moon's surface. They gathered rocks in their pockets, described their surroundings (a magnificent desolation, according to one astronaut), spoke by phone to the president, and planted a flag in lunar soil. The voyage was hailed as man's most awesome achievement. I had seen full-page photographs in the *Globe*, of the astronauts in their inflated costumes, and read about what certain people in Boston had been doing at the exact moment the astronauts landed, on a Sunday afternoon. A man said that he was operating a swan boat with a radio pressed to his ear; a woman had been baking rolls for her grandchildren.

The woman bellowed, "A flag on the moon, boy! I heard it on the radio! Isn't that splendid?"

"Yes, madame."

But she was not satisfied with my reply. Instead she commanded, "Say 'splendid'!"

I was both baffled and somewhat insulted by the request. It

reminded me of the way I was taught multiplication tables as a child, repeating after the master, sitting cross-legged, without shoes or pencils, on the floor of my one-room Tollygunge school. It also reminded me of my wedding, when I had re-peated endless Sanskrit verses after the priest, verses I barely understood, which joined me to my wife. I said nothing.

"Say 'splendid'!" the woman bellowed once again.

"Splendid," I murmured. I had to repeat the word a second time at the top of my lungs, so she could hear. I am soft-spoken by nature and was especially reluctant to raise my voice to an elderly woman whom I had met only moments ago, but she did not appear to be offended. If anything the reply pleased her because her next command was:

"Go see the room!"

I rose from the bench and mounted the narrow carpeted staircase. There were five doors, two on either side of an equally narrow hallway, and one at the opposite end. Only one door was partly open. The room contained a twin bed under a sloping ceiling, a brown oval rug, a basin with an exposed pipe, and a chest of drawers. One door, painted white, led to a closet, another to a toilet and a tub. The walls were covered with gray and ivory striped paper. The window was open; net curtains stirred in the breeze. I lifted them away and inspected the view: a small back yard, with a few fruit trees and an empty clothesline. I was satisfied. From the bottom of the stairs I heard the woman demand, "What is your decision?"

When I returned to the foyer and told her, she picked up the leather change purse on the table, opened the clasp, fished about with her fingers, and produced a key on a thin wire hoop. She informed me that there was a kitchen at the back of the house, accessible through the parlor. I was welcome to use the stove as long as I left it as I found it. Sheets and towels were provided, but keeping them clean was my own responsibility. The rent was due Friday mornings on the ledge above the piano keys. "And no lady visitors!"

"I am a married man, madame." It was the first time I had announced this fact to anyone.

But she had not heard. "No lady visitors!" she insisted. She introduced herself as Mrs. Croft.

My wife's name was Mala. The marriage had been arranged by my older brother and his wife. I regarded the proposition with neither objection nor enthusiasm. It was a duty expected of me, as it was expected of every man. She was the daughter of a schoolteacher in Beleghata. I was told that she could cook, knit, embroider, sketch landscapes, and recite poems by Tagore, but these talents could not make up for the fact that she did not possess a fair complexion, and so a string of men had rejected her to her face. She was twenty-seven, an age when her parents had begun to fear that she would never marry, and so they were willing to ship their only child halfway across the world in order to save her from spinsterhood.

For five nights we shared a bed. Each of those nights, after applying cold cream and braiding her hair, which she tied up at the end with a black cotton string, she turned from me and wept; she missed her parents. Although I would be leaving the country in a few days, custom dictated that she was now a part of my household, and for the next six weeks she was to live with my brother and his wife, cooking, cleaning, serving tea and sweets to guests. I did nothing to console her. I lay on my own side of the bed, reading my guidebook by flashlight and anticipating my journey. At times I thought of the tiny room on the other side of the wall which had belonged to my mother. Now the room was practically empty; the wooden pallet on which she'd once slept was piled with trunks and old bedding. Nearly six years ago, before leaving for London, I had watched her die on that bed, had found her playing with her excrement in her final days. Before we cremated her I had cleaned each of her fingernails with a hairpin, and then, because my brother could not bear it, I had assumed the role of eldest son, and had touched the flame to her temple, to release her tormented soul to heaven.

The next morning I moved into the room in Mrs. Croft's house. When I unlocked the door I saw that she was sitting on the piano bench, on the same side as the previous evening. She wore the same black skirt, the same starched white blouse, and had her hands folded together the same way in her lap. She looked so much the same that I wondered if she'd spent the whole night on the bench. I put my suitcase upstairs, filled my flask with boiling water in the kitchen, and headed off to work. That evening when I came home from the university, she was still there.

"Sit down, boy!" She slapped the space beside her.

I perched beside her on the bench. I had a bag of groceries with me — more milk, more cornflakes, and more bananas, for my inspection of the kitchen earlier in the day had revealed no spare pots, pans, or cooking utensils. There were only two saucepans in the refrigerator, both containing some orange broth, and a copper kettle on the stove.

"Good evening, madame."

She asked me if I had checked the lock. I told her I had.

For a moment she was silent. Then suddenly she declared, with the equal measures of disbelief and delight as the night before, "There's an American flag on the moon, boy!"

"Yes, madame."

"A flag on the moon! Isn't that splendid?"

I nodded, dreading what I knew was coming. "Yes, madame."

"Say 'splendid'!"

This time I paused, looking to either side in case anyone were there to overhear me, though I knew perfectly well that the house was empty. I felt like an idiot. But it was a small enough thing to ask. "Splendid!" I cried out.

Within days it became our routine. In the mornings when I left for the library Mrs. Croft was either hidden away in her bedroom, on the other side of the staircase, or she was sitting on the bench, oblivious to my presence, listening to the news or classical music on the radio. But each evening when I returned the same thing happened: she slapped the bench, ordered me to sit down, declared that there was a flag on the moon, and declared that it was splendid. I said it was splendid, too, and then we sat in silence. As awkward as it was, and as endless as it felt to me then, the nightly encounter lasted only about ten minutes; inevitably she would drift off to sleep, her head falling abruptly toward her chest, leaving me free to retire to my room. By then, of course, there was no flag on the moon. The astronauts, I had read in the paper, had taken it down before flying back to Earth. But I did not have the heart to tell her.

Friday morning, when my first week's rent was due, I went to the piano in the parlor to place my money on the ledge. The piano keys were dull and discolored. When I pressed one, it made no sound at all. I had put eight one-dollar bills in an envelope and written Mrs. Croft's name on the front of it. I was not in the habit of leaving money unmarked and unattended. From where I stood I could see the profile of her tent-shaped skirt. She was sitting on the bench, listening to the radio. It seemed unnecessary to make her get up and walk all the way to the piano. I never saw her walking about, and assumed, from the cane always propped against the round table at her side, that she did so with difficulty. When I approached the bench she peered up at me and demanded:

"What is your business?"

"The rent, madame."

"On the ledge above the piano keys!"

"I have it here." I extended the envelope toward her, but her fingers, folded together in her lap, did not budge. I bowed slightly and lowered the envelope, so that it hovered just above her hands. After a moment she accepted, and nodded her head.

That night when I came home, she did not slap the bench, but out of habit I sat beside her as usual. She asked me if I had checked the lock, but she mentioned nothing about the flag on the moon. Instead she said:

"It was very kind of you!"

"I beg your pardon, madame?"

"Very kind of you!"

She was still holding the envelope in her hands.

On Sunday there was a knock on my door. An elderly woman introduced herself: she was Mrs. Croft's daughter, Helen. She walked into the room and looked at each of the walls as if for signs of change, glancing at the shirts that hung in the closet, the neckties draped over the doorknob, the box of cornflakes on the chest of drawers, the dirty bowl and spoon in the basin. She was short and thick-waisted, with cropped silver hair and bright pink lipstick. She wore a sleeveless summer dress, a row of white plastic beads, and spectacles on a chain that hung like a swing against her chest. The backs of her legs were mapped with dark blue veins, and her upper arms sagged like the flesh of a roasted eggplant. She told me she lived in Arlington, a town farther up Massachusetts Avenue. "I come once a week to bring Mother groceries. Has she sent you packing yet?"

"It is very well, madame."

"Some of the boys run screaming. But I think she likes you. You're the first boarder she's ever referred to as a gentleman."

"Not at all, madame."

She looked at me, noticing my bare feet (I still felt strange wearing shoes indoors, and always removed them before entering my room). "Are you new to Boston?"

"New to America, madame."

"From?" She raised her eyebrows.

"I am from Calcutta, India."

"Is that right? We had a Brazilian fellow, about a year ago. You'll find Cambridge a very international city."

I nodded, and began to wonder how long our conversation would last. But at that moment we heard Mrs. Croft's electrifying voice rising up the stairs. When we stepped into the hallway we heard her hollering:

"You are to come downstairs immediately!"

"What is it?" Helen hollered back.

"Immediately!"

I put on my shoes at once. Helen sighed.

We walked down the staircase. It was too narrow for us to descend side by side, so I followed Helen, who seemed to be in no hurry, and complained at one point that she had a bad knee. "Have you been walking without your cane?" Helen called out. "You know you're not supposed to walk without that cane." She paused, resting her hand on the banister, and looked back at me. "She slips sometimes."

For the first time Mrs. Croft seemed vulnerable. I pictured her on the floor in front of the bench, flat on her back, staring at the ceiling, her feet pointing in opposite directions. But when we reached the bottom of the staircase she was sitting there as usual, her hands folded together in her lap. Two grocery bags were at her feet. When we stood before her she did not slap the bench, or ask us to sit down. She glared.

"What is it, Mother?"

"It's improper!"

"What's improper?"

"It is improper for a lady and gentleman who are not married to one another to hold a private conversation without a chaperone!"

Helen said she was sixty-eight years old, old enough to be my mother, but Mrs. Croft insisted that Helen and I speak to each other downstairs, in the parlor. She added that it was also improper for a lady of Helen's station to reveal her age, and to wear a dress so high above the ankle.

"For your information, Mother, it's 1969. What would you do if you actually left the house one day and saw a girl in a miniskirt?"

Mrs. Croft sniffed. "I'd have her arrested."

Helen shook her head and picked up one of the grocery bags. I picked up the other one, and followed her through the parlor and into the kitchen. The bags were filled with cans of soup, which Helen opened up one by one with a few cranks of a can opener. She tossed the old soup in the saucepans into the sink, rinsed the pans under the tap, filled them with soup from the newly opened cans, and put them back in the refrigerator. "A few years ago she could still open the cans herself," Helen said. "She hates that I do it for her now. But the piano killed her hands." She put on her spectacles, glanced at the cupboards, and spotted my tea bags. "Shall we have a cup?"

I filled the kettle on the stove. "I beg your pardon, madame. The piano?"

"She used to give lessons. For forty years. It was how she raised us after my father died." Helen put her hands on her hips, staring at the open refrigerator. She reached into the back, pulled out a wrapped stick of butter, frowned, and tossed it into the garbage. "That ought to do it," she said, and put the unopened cans of soup in the cupboard. I sat at the table and watched as Helen washed the dirty dishes, tied up the garbage bag, watered a spider plant over the sink, and poured boiling water into two cups. She handed one to me without milk, the string of the tea bag trailing over the side, and sat down at the table.

"Excuse me, madame, but is it enough?"

Helen took a sip of her tea. Her lipstick left a smiling pink stain on the inside rim of the cup. "Is what enough?"

"The soup in the pans. Is it enough food for Mrs. Croft?"

"She won't eat anything else. She stopped eating solids after she turned one hundred. That was, let's see, three years ago."

I was mortified. I had assumed Mrs. Croft was in her eighties, perhaps as old as ninety. I had never known a person who had lived for over a century. That this person was a widow who lived alone mortified me further still. It was widowhood that had driven my own mother insane. My father, who worked as a clerk at the General Post Office of Calcutta, died of encephalitis when I was sixteen. My mother refused to adjust to life without him; instead she sank deeper into a world of darkness from which neither I, nor my brother, nor concerned relatives, nor psychiatric clinics on Rashbihari Avenue could save her. What pained me most was to see her so unguarded, to hear her burp after meals or expel gas in front of company without the slightest embarrassment. After my father's death my brother abandoned his schooling and began to work in the jute mill he would eventually manage, in order to keep the household running. And so it was my job to sit by my mother's feet and study for my exams as she counted and recounted the bracelets on her arm as if they were the beads of an abacus. We tried to keep an eye on her. Once she had wandered half naked to the tram depot before we were able to bring her inside again.

"I am happy to warm Mrs. Croft's soup in the evenings," I suggested, removing the tea bag from my cup and squeezing out the liquor. "It is no trouble."

Helen looked at her watch, stood up, and poured the rest of her tea into the sink. "I wouldn't if I were you. That's the sort of thing that would kill her altogether."

That evening, when Helen had gone back to Arlington and Mrs. Croft and I were alone again, I began to worry. Now that I knew how very old she was, I worried that something would happen to her in the middle of the night, or when I was out during the day. As vigorous as her voice was, and imperious as she seemed, I knew that even a scratch or a cough could kill a person that old; each day she lived, I knew, was something of a miracle. Although Helen had seemed friendly enough, a small part of me worried that she might accuse me of negligence if anything were to happen. Helen didn't seem worried. She came and went, bringing soup for Mrs. Croft, one Sunday after the next.

In this manner the six weeks of that summer passed. I came home each evening, after my hours at the library, and spent a few minutes on the piano bench with Mrs. Croft. I gave her a bit of my company, and assured her that I had checked the lock, and told her that the flag on the moon was splendid. Some evenings I sat beside her long after she had drifted off to sleep, still in awe of how many years she had spent on this earth. At times I tried to picture the world she had been born into, in 1866 — a world, I imagined, filled with women in long black skirts, and chaste conversations in the parlor. Now, when I looked at her hands with their swollen knuckles folded together in her lap, I imagined them smooth and slim, striking the piano keys. At times I came downstairs before going to sleep, to make sure she was sitting upright on the bench, or was safe in her bedroom. On Fridays I made sure to put the rent in her hands. There was nothing I could do for her beyond these simple gestures. I was not her son, and apart from those eight dollars, I owed her nothing.

At the end of August, Mala's passport and green card were ready. I received a telegram with her flight information; my brother's house in Calcutta had no telephone. Around that time I also received a letter from her, written only a few days after we had parted. There was no salutation; addressing me by name would have assumed an intimacy we had not yet discovered. It contained only a few lines. "I write in English in preparation for the journey. Here I am very much lonely. Is it very cold there. Is there snow. Yours, Mala."

I was not touched by her words. We had spent only a handful of days in each other's company. And yet we were bound together; for six weeks she had worn an iron bangle on her wrist, and applied vermilion powder to the part in her hair, to signify to the world that she was a bride. In those six weeks I regarded her arrival as I would the arrival of a coming month, or season — something inevitable, but meaningless at the time. So little did I know her that, while details of her face sometimes rose to my memory, I could not conjure up the whole of it.

A few days after receiving the letter, as I was walking to work in the morning, I saw an Indian woman on the other side of Massachusetts Avenue, wearing a sari with its free end nearly dragging on the footpath, and pushing a child in a stroller. An American woman with a small black dog on a leash was walking to one side of her. Suddenly the dog began barking. From the other side of the street I watched as the Indian woman, startled, stopped in her path, at which point the dog leapt up and seized the end of the sari between its teeth. The American woman scolded the dog, appeared to apologize, and walked quickly away, leaving the Indian woman to fix her sari in the middle of the footpath, and quiet her crying child. She did not see me standing there, and eventually she continued on her way. Such a mishap, I realized that morning, would soon be my concern. It was my duty to take care of Mala, to welcome her and protect her. I would have to buy her her first pair of snow boots, her first winter coat. I would have to tell her which streets to avoid, which way the traffic came, tell her to wear her sari so that the free end did not drag on the footpath. A five-mile separation from her parents, I recalled with some irritation, had caused her to weep.

Unlike Mala, I was used to it all by then: used to cornflakes and milk, used to Helen's visits, used to sitting on the bench with Mrs. Croft. The only thing I was not used to was Mala. Nevertheless I did what I had to do. I went to the housing office at MIT and found a furnished apartment a few blocks away, with a double bed and a private kitchen and bath, for forty dollars a week. One last Friday I handed Mrs. Croft eight one-dollar bills in an envelope, brought my suitcase downstairs, and informed her that I was moving. She put my key into her change purse. The last thing she asked me to do was hand her the cane propped against the table, so that she could walk to the door and lock it behind me. "Good-bye, then," she said, and retreated back into the house. I did not expect any display of emotion, but I was disappointed all the same. I was only a boarder, a man who paid her a bit of money and passed in and out of her home for six weeks. Compared to a century, it was no time at all.

At the airport I recognized Mala immediately. The free end of her sari did not drag on the floor, but was draped in a sign of bridal modesty over her head, just as it had draped my mother until the day my father died. Her thin brown arms were stacked with gold bracelets, a small red circle was painted on her forehead, and the edges of her feet were tinted with a decorative red dye. I did not embrace her, or kiss her, or take her hand. Instead I asked her, speaking Bengali for the first time in America, if she was hungry.

She hesitated, then nodded yes.

I told her I had prepared some egg curry at home. "What did they give you to eat on the plane?"

"I didn't eat."

"All the way from Calcutta?"

"The menu said oxtail soup."

"But surely there were other items."

"The thought of eating an ox's tail made me lose my appetite."

When we arrived home, Mala opened up one of her suitcases, and presented me with two pullover sweaters, both made with bright blue wool, which she had knitted in the course of our separation, one with a V neck, the other covered with cables. I tried them on; both were tight under the arms. She had also brought me two new pairs of drawstring pajamas, a letter from my brother, and a packet of loose Darjeeling tea.

I had no present for her apart from the egg curry. We sat at a bare table, each of us staring at our plates. We ate with our hands, another thing I had not yet done in America.

"The house is nice," she said. "Also the egg curry." With her left hand she held the end of her sari to her chest, so it would not slip off her head.

"I don't know many recipes."

She nodded, peeling the skin off each of her potatoes before eating them. At one point the sari slipped to her shoulders. She readjusted it at once.

"There is no need to cover your head," I said. "I don't mind. It doesn't matter here."

She kept it covered anyway.

I waited to get used to her, to her presence at my side, at my table and in my bed, but a week later we were still strangers. I still was not used to coming home to an apartment that smelled of steamed rice, and finding that the basin in the bathroom was always wiped clean, our two toothbrushes lying side by side, a cake of Pears soap from India resting in the soap dish. I was not used to the fragrance of the coconut oil she rubbed every other night into her scalp, or the delicate sound her bracelets made as she moved about the apartment. In the mornings she was always awake before I was. The first morning when I came into the kitchen she had heated up the leftovers and set a plate with a spoonful of salt on its edge on the table, assuming I would eat rice for breakfast, as most Bengali husbands did. I told her cereal would do, and the next morning when I came into the kitchen she had already poured the cornflakes into my bowl. One morning she walked with me down Massachusetts Avenue to MIT, where I gave her a short tour of the campus. On the way we stopped at a hardware store and I made a copy of the key, so that she could let herself into the apartment. The next morning before I left for work she asked me for a few dollars. I parted with them reluctantly, but I knew that this, too, was now normal. When I came home from work there was a potato peeler in the kitchen drawer, and a tablecloth on the table, and chicken curry made with fresh garlic and ginger on the stove. We did not have a television in those days. After dinner I read the newspaper, while Mala sat at the kitchen table, working on a cardigan for herself with more of the bright blue wool, or writing letters home.

At the end of our first week, on Friday, I suggested going out. Mala set down her knitting and disappeared into the bathroom. When she emerged I regretted the suggestion; she had put on a clean silk sari and extra bracelets, and coiled her hair with a flattering side part on top of her head. She was prepared as if for a party, or at the very least for the cinema, but I had no such destination in mind. The evening air was balmy. We walked several blocks down Massachusetts Avenue, looking into the windows of restaurants and shops. Then, without thinking, I led her down the quiet street where for so many nights I had walked alone.

"This is where I lived before you came," I said, stopping at Mrs. Croft's chain-link fence.

"In such a big house?"

"I had a small room upstairs. At the back."

"Who else lives there?"

"A very old woman."

"With her family?"

"Alone."

"But who takes care of her?"

I opened the gate. "For the most part she takes care of herself."

I wondered if Mrs. Croft would remember me; I wondered

if she had a new boarder to sit with her on the bench each evening. When I pressed the bell I expected the same long wait as that day of our first meeting, when I did not have a key. But this time the door was opened almost immediately, by Helen. Mrs. Croft was not sitting on the bench. The bench was gone.

"Hello there," Helen said, smiling with her bright pink lips at Mala. "Mother's in the parlor. Will you be visiting awhile?"

"As you wish, madame."

"Then I think I'll run to the store, if you don't mind. She had a little accident. We can't leave her alone these days, not even for a minute."

I locked the door after Helen and walked into the parlor. Mrs. Croft was lying flat on her back, her head on a peach-colored cushion, a thin white quilt spread over her body. Her hands were folded together on top of her chest. When she saw me she pointed at the sofa, and told me to sit down. I took my place as directed, but Mala wandered over to the piano and sat on the bench, which was now positioned where it belonged.

"I broke my hip!" Mrs. Croft announced, as if no time had passed.

"Oh dear, madame."

"I fell off the bench!"

"I am so sorry, madame."

"It was the middle of the night! Do you know what I did, boy?"

I shook my head.

"I called the police!"

She stared up at the ceiling and grinned sedately, exposing a crowded row of long gray teeth. Not one was missing. "What do you say to that, boy?"

As stunned as I was, I knew what I had to say. With no hesitation at all, I cried out, "Splendid!"

Mala laughed then. Her voice was full of kindness, her eyes bright with amusement. I had never heard her laugh before, and it was loud enough so that Mrs. Croft had heard, too. She turned to Mala and glared.

"Who is she, boy?"

"She is my wife, madame."

Mrs. Croft pressed her head at an angle against the cushion to get a better look. "Can you play the piano?"

"No, madame," Mala replied.

"Then stand up!"

Mala rose to her feet, adjusting the end of her sari over her head and holding it to her chest, and, for the first time since her arrival, I felt sympathy. I remembered my first days in London, learning how to take the Tube to Russell Square, riding an escalator for the first time, being unable to understand that when the man cried "piper" it meant "paper," being unable to decipher, for a whole year, that the conductor said "mind the gap" as the train pulled away from each station. Like me, Mala had traveled far from home, not knowing where she was going, or what she would find, for no reason other than to be my wife. As strange as it seemed, I knew in my heart that one day her death would affect me, and stranger still, that mine would affect her. I wanted somehow to explain this to Mrs. Croft, who was still scrutinizing Mala from top to toe with what seemed to be placid disdain. I wondered if Mrs. Croft had ever seen a woman in a sari, with a dot painted on her forehead and bracelets stacked on her wrists. I wondered what she would object to. I wondered if she could see the red dye still vivid on Mala's feet, all but obscured by the bottom edge of her sari. At last Mrs. Croft declared, with the equal measures of disbelief and delight I knew well:

"She is a perfect lady!"

Now it was I who laughed. I did so quietly, and Mrs. Croft did not hear me. But Mala had heard, and, for the first time, we looked at each other and smiled.

I like to think of that moment in Mrs. Croft's parlor as the moment when the distance between Mala and me began to lessen. Although we were not yet fully in love, I like to think of the months that followed as a honeymoon of sorts. Together we explored the city and met other Bengalis, some of whom are still friends today. We discovered that a man named Bill sold fresh fish on Prospect Street, and that a shop in Harvard Square called Cardullo's sold bay leaves and cloves. In the evenings we walked to the Charles River to watch sailboats drift across the water, or had ice cream cones in Harvard Yard. We bought an Instamatic camera with which to document our life together, and I took pictures of her posing in front of the Prudential building, so that she could send them to her parents. At night we kissed, shy at first but quickly bold, and discovered pleasure and solace in each other's arms. I told her about my voyage on the SS *Roma*, and about Finsbury Park and the YMCA, and my evenings on the bench with Mrs. Croft. When I told her stories about my mother, she wept. It was Mala who consoled me when, reading the *Globe* one evening, I came across Mrs. Croft's obituary. I had not thought of her in several months — by then those six weeks of the summer were already a remote interlude in my past — but when I learned of her death I was stricken, so much so that when Mala looked up from her knitting she found me staring at the wall, the newspaper neglected in my lap, unable to speak. Mrs. Croft's was the first death I mourned in America, for hers was the first life I had admired; she had left this world at last, ancient and alone, never to return.

As for me, I have not strayed much farther. Mala and I live in a town about twenty miles from Boston, on a tree-lined street much like Mrs. Croft's, in a house we own, with a garden that saves us from buying tomatoes in summer, and room for guests. We are American citizens now, so that we can collect social security when it is time. Though we visit Calcutta every few years, and bring back more drawstring pajamas and Darjeeling tea, we have decided to grow old here. I work in a small college library. We have a son who attends Harvard University. Mala no longer drapes the end of her sari over her head, or weeps at night for her parents, but occasionally she weeps for our son. So we drive to Cambridge to visit him, or bring him home for a weekend, so that he can eat rice with us with his hands, and speak in Bengali, things we sometimes worry he will no longer do after we die.

Whenever we make that drive, I always make it a point to take Massachusetts Avenue, in spite of the traffic. I barely recognize the buildings now, but each time I am there I return instantly to those six weeks as if they were only the other day, and I slow down and point to Mrs. Croft's street, saying to my son, here was my first home in America, where I lived with a woman who was 103. "Remember?" Mala says, and smiles, amazed, as I am, that there was ever a time that we were strangers. My son always expresses his astonishment, not at Mrs. Croft's age, but at how little I paid in rent, a fact nearly as inconceivable to him as a flag on the moon was to a woman born in 1866. In my son's eyes I see the ambition that had first hurled me across the world. In a few years he will graduate and pave his way, alone and unprotected. But I remind myself that he has a father who is still living, a mother who is happy and strong. Whenever he is discouraged, I tell him that if I can survive on three continents, then there is no obstacle he cannot conquer. While the astronauts, heroes forever, spent mere hours on the moon, I have remained in this new world for nearly thirty years. I know that my achievement is quite ordinary. I am not the only man to seek his fortune far from home, and certainly I am not the first. Still, there are times I am bewildered by each mile I have traveled, each meal I have eaten, each person I have known, each room in which I have slept. As ordinary as it all appears, there are times when it is beyond my imagination.